A gunshot exploded in the night...

Beth started at the noise.

Then Cole dived at her, propelling her down the stairs and into the sheltered space beside them.

It wasn't until the second blast, until she heard a brick splinter in the wall above her, that it dawned on her that someone was shooting at *them*.

Her heart began hammering faster. But there was only silence.

They stayed right where they were, Cole's body pressing hers to the building. She could feel the warmth of his breath fanning her skin, and the sensation sent a tiny ripple of desire through her, taking her completely by surprise.

It seemed bizarre that she could feel the attraction. They'd almost been killed, and she couldn't stop shaking. But she was aware, oh, so aware, of her body heat mingling with his.

She moved her head to look at Cole. He was watching her—as if he knew exactly what she was thinking....

Dear Reader,

I've always been interested in the workings of the human mind, which undoubtedly explains why I majored in psychology and spent many years working with psychiatrists.

In *The Missing Hour*, heroine Beth Gregory goes to great lengths to help her repressed memory surface. But when it does, she wishes with all her heart that it hadn't.

Remembering seeing the murder of someone she loved is bad enough. Remembering that the killer was her own father is a hundred times worse.

This is a book about relationships—the good, the bad and the ugly. And about the fact that, sometimes, it's hard to distinguish one type from another until it's too late.

The Missing Hour is my twenty-sixth novel for Harlequin. I hope you enjoy reading it.

Warmest regards,

Dawn Stewardson

P.S. For those of you who know that I often draw on my own pets to create animal characters, yes, I do have two cats. But their names are Yeats and Salem, not Bogey and Bacall.

The Missing Hour
Dawn Stewardson

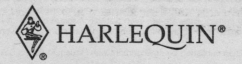

HARLEQUIN®

TORONTO • NEW YORK • LONDON
AMSTERDAM • PARIS • SYDNEY • HAMBURG
STOCKHOLM • ATHENS • TOKYO • MILAN • MADRID
PRAGUE • WARSAW • BUDAPEST • AUCKLAND

To my mother and father,
who like mysteries.
And to John, always.

ISBN 0-373-22470-2

THE MISSING HOUR

The Niebuhrs' House •

• Esther Voise's House

Mark Niebuhr's Office •

Tranby Avenue

Bedford Road

Bloor Street West

Avenue Road

CAST OF CHARACTERS

Beth Gregory—She'd had traumatic amnesia for twenty-two years. Now that she remembered, could her memory possibly be wrong?

Cole Radford—He thought he'd signed on to investigate a twenty-two-year-old murder—but his greatest challenge became keeping his client alive.

Glen Gregory—Beth's father had no motive for murdering Beth's aunt—or did he?

Angela Gregory—She'd discovered her daughter crying by her sister's body. Why hadn't she called the police immediately?

Dr. Mark Niebuhr—Larisa's husband revered his wife's memory. But when Cole and Beth discovered the truth about Larisa, they had to wonder—why?

Larisa Niebuhr—Beth's aunt died before Beth's eyes. What secrets had she taken with her?

Frank Abbott—The retired police detective had never believed Larisa was killed by an unknown intruder.

Esther Voise—The Niebuhrs' neighbor had seen almost all of the murder suspects—including the mystery man.

Prologue

The dust in the attic was tickling Beth's nose, but she barely noticed. She was too busy watching Aunt Larisa pull treasure after treasure from a trunk and toss them onto a growing rainbow of color on the old couch.

"There, honey," she finally said. "Think that's enough for some good dress-up?"

Beth nodded, feeling bubbly inside. She loved it when Mommy left her at Aunt Larisa's house. They always spent every minute playing.

Mommy said that was because Aunt Larisa didn't have any kids of her own to play with, but the *why* didn't matter. Beth just liked it—specially the way Aunt Larisa let her do things she never got to do at home, like put on real makeup.

Oh, they had to wash it off before Mommy came to pick her up, but it was still lots of fun. And it felt good here. Specially when Aunt Larisa hugged her and said she was her absolutely favorite niece.

Sometimes Uncle Mark was home and heard that. Then he'd laugh and say Beth was their *only* niece. But she didn't care if he teased. She knew she'd still be Aunt Larisa's absolutely favorite no matter what.

"Okay, honey." Her aunt gave her a warm smile. "Which one do you want to try first? How about this red velvet number? You'd look like Santa."

That made her laugh. Aunt Larisa could be awfully silly.

"Santa's an old man with a long white beard," she pointed out. "And it's July. I don't think he wears his red suit in July."

"No? Well, don't be too sure about that, because Mrs. Claus is a personal friend of mine, and she once told me..."

"Told you what?"

"Just a sec. I thought I heard a noise downstairs."

Beth scrunched up her face so she could listen real hard, but she didn't hear anything. She was just going to say so when she heard a creak.

"Mark?" Aunt Larisa called.

Something in her voice made goose bumps pop up on Beth's bare arms.

"Mark, is that you?"

The house was silent for a minute. Then there was another creak.

Beth swallowed hard. Her aunt looked scared, and that was very frightening. If *she* wasn't sure who was in the house...

"It *has* to be Uncle Mark," she said quietly. "Because we checked all the locks before we came up here, right?"

"Uh-huh." Aunt Larisa always checked the locks. And Beth always helped her.

"Okay, you stay right here, honey, and be quiet as a mouse. Hey, you know, maybe *that's* what's making the noise. Maybe there's a mouse downstairs. I'll just go check, and be right back."

Her heart beating fast, Beth watched Aunt Larisa hurry downstairs. Then she waited, straining her ears but not hearing another sound.

Finally, she couldn't stay in the attic by herself for a second longer. As quietly as she could, she crept down the stairs.

Aunt Larisa had closed the door at the bottom, so Beth stopped on the last step and pressed her ear to the wood. She could hear her aunt talking to someone, and she sounded awful scared.

Awful scared herself, Beth cracked the door open. Only a tiny bit. Only enough to peek along the hall. She peered through the crack—and was plunged into a black void.

Chapter One

Beth Gregory woke with a start, her heart pounding.

Moonbeams, streaming in through the skylight, softened the blackness to silver. She was safe in her bedroom; it had only been the nightmare again.

But it was so vividly real, it had left her shaking inside—almost unable to believe she was actually a thirty-year-old woman, not the eight-year-old child she'd been that day.

Sitting up, she turned on the bedside lamp to keep the demons of the dark entirely at bay. Bogey and Bacall grumbled a few throaty cat complaints from the end of the bed, while she sat gazing at shadows and trying to make sense of things.

Did these nightmares she'd been having mean that when she'd gone down those stairs she really *had* witnessed Larisa's murder?

For what had to be the millionth time, she wondered how many people had asked her if she had. And how often she'd asked herself.

But she didn't know the answer now, any more than she had all those years ago, because the nightmares invariably ended with her plunging into that black void the moment she peered through the crack.

And, consciously, she'd never remembered anything from the moment she'd cracked that door open until she'd realized her mother was there with her, hugging her and crying hysterically.

It was as if time had stood still. Yet, in reality, she'd spent at least an hour sitting on the attic stairs—however much time had passed between her aunt's murder and when her mother arrived to pick her up.

Switching off the lamp, she scrunched down beneath the blankets again and lay staring up at the moon. The bedroom skylight was one of the things she loved most about her apartment.

Its louvered blind was on a timer that slid it closed before dawn, so the sun didn't come streaming in and wake her. But before she went to sleep at night, she could watch the stars above.

After a minute or two she closed her eyes, even though she could almost never get back to sleep after one of the nightmares. They left her brain working in overdrive, trying to come up with a surefire way of making them stop.

Logic said they were manifestations of her long-repressed memories trying to surface. And if they just could, maybe it would do the trick. With that in mind, she'd made every effort to help them.

First, she'd tried to talk to her mother about Larisa's murder. But that had been a disaster, with her mother ending up in tears.

Finding her sister's body, she'd explained, had been the worst moment of her entire life. And even after all this time, she still couldn't bear to talk about it.

So, ghoulish as it had made her feel, Beth had

gone through old microfilms of the *Toronto Star* and the *Sun,* photocopying anything and everything related to the murder.

Much of it was pure speculation, because the police hadn't released many details. And no matter how often she reread the articles, they hadn't helped her remember a thing about that missing hour. Not so far, at any rate.

She lay in the darkness for a little longer, phrases from the articles drifting through her head. Then she gave up and got out of bed, eliciting another round of complaints from the cats.

Telling them to go back to sleep, she headed for the kitchen, flicking on lights as she went.

Aside from her bedroom, with its tiny two-piece en suite bathroom, and the main bathroom, the apartment was a loftlike open space. Her living-dining room sprawled across its width, with only a counter unit defining where the kitchen began.

Her office, which lay beyond the living area, was separated from it by nothing more than a wall of glass bricks—and even that only extended about three-quarters of the way across the space and just partway to the ceiling.

She liked the openness; the lack of closed doors made her feel safe.

And was that, she asked herself, because she'd once seen something horrible happen through an almost closed door? Or were her nightmares merely some sort of perverse self-torture?

Whichever, she was starting to think she needed help, because the nightmares were really messing up her mind.

In the kitchen, she made a pot of coffee and filled

her favorite mug. Then, as if drawn by a magnet, she carried the coffee into her office. Taking the file folder out of the bottom drawer, she opened it onto the desk and let her gaze slowly sweep bits and pieces of the first photocopy.

Police believe the murderer removed the screen from an unlocked kitchen window to gain entry, then left via the back door.

And left it unlocked. That was how Beth's mother had gotten in when nobody answered her knocks— one of the details that *had* been mentioned somewhere in the articles.

Turning to the next one, Beth skimmed a paragraph from it.

Mrs. Niebuhr's body was discovered by her sister, who had arrived to pick up her daughter. The child was playing in the basement of the house, and police say she had no idea what had happened.

She hadn't, of course, been playing in the basement. And the police were never certain whether she'd seen the murder or not. That statement had simply been issued for her protection—just as laws had prevented the news media from publishing her mother's name, to protect the identity of her child.

Beth glanced at the article again and picked up where she'd left off. ...*she had no idea what had happened. Police believe the killer was unaware of her presence in the house.*

The killer had been unaware of her presence. But had she been more aware of his than she could recall?

Slowly, she shook her head, still amazed that a child could so thoroughly repress something. She'd done a bang-up job of it, though.

At the time, there'd been a surprising number of specialists interested in traumatic amnesia. And it had seemed as if every single one of them had come crawling out of the woodwork.

Psychiatrists and psychologists and a whole ream of other "ists" had poked and prodded at her eight-year-old mind. She'd even been hypnotized, in an attempt to determine whether she'd actually seen the murder.

But when none of the experts could make her remember, the police gave up hope of having an eyewitness. Ultimately, the case remained unsolved—the murderer assumed to be an unknown intruder who'd stabbed Larisa to death when she'd confronted him.

Beth took a sip of coffee, then turned to the next article and forced her tired eyes to focus.

The police are appealing to the public for help in identifying Larisa Niebuhr's murderer. Anyone who saw a stranger in the vicinity of Tranby Avenue on July 27, between 10:00 a.m. and 12:30 p.m., is asked to call Fifty-nine Division at 555-5959.

July 27. Her gaze lingered on the date. In only about six weeks it would be July 27 of *this* year—twenty-two years after the fact.

She sat back, letting her thoughts drift. The police appeal had resulted in numerous calls from the public. But none of the callers had seen anyone near Tranby Avenue with blood on his clothes. And surely there'd have been so much blood....

Blood. The word began oozing through her mind. Then a bolt of brilliant crimson flashed before her eyes—and sent a chill up her spine.

UNDER NORMAL circumstances, Beth loved being in her uncle's penthouse. The day she graduated from interior design, he'd hired her to redecorate his living room—her first paying assignment—and every time she was here she felt good about herself.

At least, every time until this morning. Now, watching Mark pace the room, she desperately wished she hadn't come.

He'd never remarried, and she suspected it was because he'd never completely gotten over Larisa's death. With that possibility in mind, after she'd decided she definitely *did* need help, she'd debated for days on end whether to ask him for it—and it looked as if she'd made the wrong decision.

Finally, he sank onto the couch opposite her. "I'm afraid I can't do it, Beth."

"I understand," she said quietly. "Listening to me talk about that day would be too hard on you. I'm sorry. I shouldn't have asked."

He ran his fingers through his hair—silvery gray now but still thick and meticulously styled to give him a truly lionlike look.

"No, asking was okay," he said. "And after all these years I could handle the listening. The problem is that you're my niece. Taking on a relative as a patient wouldn't be ethical."

"Aah," she murmured, relieved the problem wasn't that she'd upset him. "Not ethical. Does that mean it's completely against the rules or just kind of dicey?

"I'm not a *blood* relative," she added when he hesitated. "Only one by marriage."

"You're as close as a blood relative."

She smiled a little. She'd always been glad he

hadn't let their relationship slip away after the murder. He'd spent a lot of time with her during her growing up years—especially after her parents had separated.

"I'll refer you to someone you'll like," he said. "I don't want to bother her on a Sunday, but I'll call her first thing in the morning."

It was obvious from Mark's expression that he wanted to help her, that he was only suggesting she see someone else because ethics suggested he should. Since ethics were the least of Beth's worries at the moment, she said, "Mark, I like *you*. And I want someone I can trust to not try forcing me. That's what they all did after it happened—tried to *make* me remember. And it's what I've been doing to myself since the nightmares started. But I'm still not positive there's even anything *to* remember, so I just want help with going slowly."

"Any competent psychiatrist would help with that."

"But I don't want *any* psychiatrist. After the murder… Well, let's just say I've had more than enough of strangers trying to pry out my innermost secrets. I'd feel so much better with you. And I wouldn't exactly be a patient. I simply need someone to talk to about the nightmares."

"Beth… Look, as a psychiatrist, I should be all in favor of your doing that. But as your uncle, I'm going to warn you there's an inherent risk.

"If you did repress something, you did so because it was too awful to deal with consciously. And if you force yourself to remember, slowly or not, there's no guarantee your nightmares will disappear. In fact, you could end up with worse ones."

"Yes, I know." Lately, she'd read a fair bit about repressed memories—enough to learn that trying to recall them could be dangerous.

"But I think I've got to take that chance," she continued, "because there's something else. Recently I've started having memory flashes, too."

"Memory flashes?" Mark leaned forward. "Exactly what do you mean?"

"Well, they're hard to describe because they're really nothing. I mean, I know they're something from the past, but they're mostly just color."

"What color?"

"Usually red and white. Sometimes green."

She wondered if he'd try to make a joke about Christmas, but he didn't say a word—merely eyed her so intently it made her nervous.

"And you think they're related to the murder?" he asked at last.

"Yes."

"What makes you believe that?"

"I don't know. I just do."

When he said nothing more, she rose and wandered across to the wall of floor-to-ceiling windows that overlooked Lake Ontario. To the right there was only choppy gray water dotted with sailboats. To the left was the downtown skyline, anchored partway along by the CN Tower.

"Have you told your mother about the nightmares? And these flashes?"

She turned away from the windows and shook her head. "You know how she is. She'd get upset, and then she'd drive herself crazy worrying."

"What about your father?"

"No...no, I haven't mentioned them to him, either.'' She was surprised Mark would even ask. Her father had lived in Alberta for so long that when he'd moved back last year they'd barely known each other. Since then, they'd been making a point of getting together every few weeks, but she didn't really confide in him.

''I've only told a couple of people,'' she offered when Mark remained silent.

''Wendy?'' he guessed.

''Of course. This is the sort of thing best friends are for.''

''And what did she say?''

''She mostly just listened and sympathized. And told me to call her if I was upset, no matter how late it was. Then, when I was trying to decide if I should talk to you about it, she encouraged me. And I've told Brian, too.''

''Oh? And his reaction was…?''

''He made his moving-in offer again—so I wouldn't be waking up from the nightmares alone.''

Mark smiled wryly. ''I take it you said thanks but no thanks again?''

''Uh-huh. I like living alone. I think it's an only-child thing.''

''Really? That's a new one to me,'' he teased. ''Maybe we should write a paper about it.''

''Maybe,'' she agreed, although they both knew her living alone had nothing to do with her being an only child. Old-fashioned as it might be, she'd never lived with a man. And she wouldn't feel right about making any sort of commitment with Brian until she felt more certain that he was her Mr. Forever.

When Mark was silent, she knew he was waiting

for her to say something more about Brian. But he wasn't what she wanted to discuss.

"Did you tell him you were coming here today?" Mark finally asked.

She nodded. "He didn't think it was a very good idea. He's not a believer in repressed memories—says it doesn't make sense that a person could forget about something as traumatic as seeing a murder. And even buying that as a possibility, he can't see why the memory would surface years later."

"A lot of people find it a difficult concept. The human mind is far more complicated than they realize. And when it comes to your case…"

Mark fell silent again and simply sat gazing across the room. Finally, he said, "All right, If you're determined to recover that memory, I'll try to help you."

His words sent a ripple of relief through her. She didn't know if she could have gone to a stranger.

"Here's what we'll do," he continued. "We'll start right now and talk more about what's been happening. Then we'll get together every evening we can. We won't consider it therapy and we won't meet in my office. You'll come here, and we'll just be an uncle and niece talking about a problem."

"Thank you," she murmured, trying to ignore the anxiety that was tinging her relief.

What if she *was* making a mistake? What if, as Brian had suggested, she'd be smarter to do nothing—to simply weather the nightmares and assume they'd eventually stop?

She couldn't do that, though. Her need to know

exactly what she'd seen, all those years ago, was more compelling than her fear of where this might lead.

"READY?" MARK ASKED, sitting down in the chair that faced Beth's.

She nodded and leaned back.

"You seem tense tonight."

"A little." But who wouldn't be? They'd started these "sessions"—for lack of a better word—over a month ago. And any time now she was going to remember what had happened during the missing hour.

Her nightmares had increased in frequency, from once or twice a week to almost every night. And Mark said that was because she was getting nearer and nearer to a breakthrough.

"All right," he said quietly, "close your eyes and start letting your memory paint a picture. And let's get you breathing properly. In...and out...deep... slow breaths."

She tried to concentrate solely on her breathing, but she couldn't stop thinking this had become very much a patient-therapist relationship. After the first few sessions, the "uncle and niece just talking" approach had gone out the window and Mark had fallen into his accustomed role of psychiatrist.

It didn't bother her, though. The slow cadence of his professional voice was reassuring, almost hypnotizing, which made it easier for her to open up.

"Good," he said, stretching the word across the space between them. "Now breathe a little more deeply...let your whole body relax.

"Let your thoughts drift back to when you were a little girl, let your memory paint a picture. And when you're ready, tell me something you see from long ago. First something about your mother, and then about your father.''

She smiled to herself. By this point, he'd given her those instructions so often they had to be etched in her brain. Close her eyes, let her memory paint a picture, tell him about her mother, tell him about her father. Then he'd follow up by asking her to elaborate on whatever she said. Or, sometimes, he'd tell her something *he* remembered about one of them.

''Breathing in now…and hold it…and out.''

''My mother,'' she finally said, ''always had the rec room strewn with pieces of her current hobby— sewing, photography, painting, whatever. She went through so many things that my father used to talk about her 'hobby du jour.'

''And he…he spent a lot of time in his study, and he'd be annoyed if my mother interrupted. So she'd send me in to get him if she needed him for something, because he almost never got annoyed with me.''

''Good…very good. Now tell me something about Larisa.''

When that brought her tension rushing back, Mark immediately said, ''Relax, Beth, just tell me something when you're ready.''

She took a few long, deep breaths, but was too anxious to close her eyes again. ''I liked being with Aunt Larisa,'' she said at last. ''Because she was almost more like another little girl than an adult.''

Her uncle nodded, looking as if his thoughts were miles away—as if he might be picturing his wife.

''And she always had so many ideas for games and things,'' Beth added. ''But one day…''

Alarm bells began going off in her head and panic welled inside her.

Mark rested his hand on hers. "You're perfectly all right. Just close your eyes again and relax."

She closed them, but relaxing was impossible.

"Deep, slow breaths. You don't have to say anything you don't want to."

But she did! Something inside her was trying to spill out, and holding it back had her heart racing a mile a minute.

"I crept down the stairs," she whispered. "I crept down the stairs and the door at the bottom was closed." She couldn't go on. Cold sweat had begun trickling down between her shoulder blades and her throat was tight with fear.

"And when you got to the closed door?"

Her heart pounding harder yet, she forced more words out. "I...I listened. And I could hear Aunt Larisa talking. She sounded afraid, so I cracked the door open just a little. And then..." The image was suddenly before her eyes—a freeze frame so unspeakable she couldn't breathe. "Oh, my Lord! It couldn't have been him!"

"THE KILLER WAS SOMEONE you knew," Mark repeated once more, sounding every bit as incredulous as he had the first three times. "The police were wrong, then. He wasn't an unknown intruder at all."

Beth stared at the carpet, so horrified she didn't know what to do or say. She shouldn't have said she'd recognized him. Not until she'd had time to think.

But the words had slipped out in her panic, and

now she had to decide what to do about Mark's knowing.

"Beth." He covered her hand with his again. "Look, I realize how incredibly upset you feel, and that's normal. To remember after all these years… But you're going to be okay, I promise."

She merely continued to sit there in silence, shaking inside. "I'm going to throw up," she whispered at last, pushing herself out of the chair and racing to the bathroom.

After every last bit of her dinner was in the toilet, she rested her forehead against the cool porcelain bowl. And with tears streaming down her face, she wished she'd never helped that memory force its way to the surface.

Now that she knew the truth, she'd rather have lived with the nightmares—because how could she live with the fact? The immediate question, though, was what was she going to do about it?

"Beth?" Mark tapped on the door. "Beth, are you all right?"

"Yes…yes, I'll be out in a minute." She pushed herself up from the floor, rinsed off her face, then opened the door.

Mark was right there, eyeing her with concern. "Come on back into the living room," he said, wrapping his arm around her shoulders. "The best thing to do is tell me exactly what you remembered. Right now. Verbalizing it will help."

As they walked down the hallway, her thoughts were racing so fast they were tumbling all over one another. How could she tell him? But after all the effort he'd put into helping her remember, how could she refuse?

She sank back into her chair; he sat down across from her once more.

"Okay," he said gently. "Slow, deep breaths. And when you're ready, tell me exactly what you remembered."

Decide, she ordered herself. But she couldn't.

"Beth?" Mark said at last. "Larisa was my wife. If you know who killed her, you've got to tell me."

His words made her feel as if a boa constrictor were wrapped around her chest—gradually squeezing more tightly. And then a wonderful realization came to her.

The killer had gotten into the house by removing a kitchen screen. Whereas, if he'd been somebody Larisa had known, he'd have simply knocked on the door. Unless...

Unless he'd only removed the screen so it would *look* as if that's how he'd gotten in.

Beth forced that thought away. The killer had been a stranger, and the memory that had surfaced simply couldn't be right. Other things from her subconscious had somehow gotten mixed in.

Or maybe that image had been nothing more than a bizarre creation of her mind. Maybe she hadn't actually seen the murder at all, but she'd been trying so hard to remember it that— Yes, there had to be *some* explanation.

She forced herself to meet Mark's gaze. "What I saw wasn't what happened that day. I think... Mark, I just don't know what to think."

"You did remember seeing the murder, though."

"Yes, but... No. I mean, I remember seeing it, but the memory wasn't right. The man I saw as the killer... Well, it just wasn't right. I can't explain it any better than that.''

"Beth? Who *did* you see as the killer?''

She hesitated, her heart pounding again, then said, "I have a question.''

"Yes?''

"About patient confidentiality.''

"Yes?''

"When we started out, you said we weren't going to consider this therapy. That we'd simply be an uncle and niece talking about a problem.''

He nodded.

"Does that mean confidentiality doesn't apply?''

"Do you want it to?''

"Yes.''

"All right,'' he said slowly. "Then it does.''

That made her breathe a little more easily, but her mouth was still cotton dry. "Why,'' she managed to say, "would I imagine the killer was someone it couldn't have been?''

"I don't know. But maybe, if you tell me who you imagined he was, we could figure that out.''

She couldn't tell him. She just couldn't. And then, her heart pounding in her ears, the words spilled out.

"My father.''

Chapter Two

Cole Radford sat behind his desk, listening closely to the story Dr. Mark Niebuhr was telling him, but his gaze kept straying to the man's niece.

Beth Gregory was an extremely attractive woman, with shaggy hair the color of summer wheat, big blue eyes and the kind of lush lips that made it hard not to stare at them.

At some point in his rambling story, Niebuhr had mentioned she was single. And that, Cole felt certain, was by choice. A woman who looked like her could probably have married a dozen times over.

It wasn't her appearance that had him eyeing her, though. It was the fact that she was radiating utter anguish. Of course, if he'd suddenly recalled seeing his father murder his aunt, he probably wouldn't be too happy the next day, either.

"So that's where we're at," Niebuhr finally concluded. "The possibility that the murderer wasn't simply an unknown intruder, but Glen Gregory."

When Cole glanced in Beth's direction again, she was looking at the floor.

"Beth?"

She met his gaze so uneasily he almost winced.

He wasn't used to making people nervous—not unless he was doing it intentionally.

"On the day of the murder, wouldn't your father have known you were with Larisa?" he asked. "That your mother was leaving you with her while she went shopping?"

Even though he'd directed the questions at Beth, Niebuhr jumped in with the answer.

"No, he probably *wouldn't* have known. Glen and Angela didn't officially call it quits until a couple of years later, but they were already leading separate lives. So Angela rarely bothered telling him how she spent her days.

"On top of which, she's always been rather..." Niebuhr paused, glancing at Beth. "I guess *erratic* would be a fair word," he continued. "She was always deciding she wanted to do something at the last minute, then calling Larisa to see if she'd look after Beth.

"That's exactly what happened the day of the murder. Angela didn't phone until after I'd left for my office. It wasn't until after the police arrived there..." Niebuhr paused again, this time taking a deep breath before he went on.

"It wasn't until after the police arrived to tell me what had happened that I learned Beth had been in the house with Larisa."

"I see," Cole said quietly. "And what about motive, as far as Glen Gregory's concerned? Would he have had any *reason* to kill your wife?"

"None that I know of."

So the man's suspicion was based solely on this recovered memory. "Why do you think the memory's finally surfaced?" he asked. "I mean, with those nightmares and all, why was it trying to surface before Beth decided to help it along?''

"Beth?" Niebuhr looked pointedly in her direction.

"The only thing I can think of," she told Cole, "is that just before they started, I was looking at a lot of snapshots of Larisa.

"When I was small, my mother was into photography for a while. And a few months ago, she said that I should see if there were any of the old albums I'd like to have. And…well, as I said, I ended up looking at a lot of pictures of Larisa."

"That would be enough to cause nightmares?" Cole asked Niebuhr.

He nodded. "Seeing the pictures would have start her thinking about Larisa—even if only subconsciously. And that might well have led to her memories trying to break through the wall she erected against them."

Cole glanced at Beth once more, wishing he knew more about the subject of recovered memories. He'd watched a television documentary on it once, but all he really recalled from that was how divided the psychiatric community was as to the validity of the concept.

"Have you talked to anyone else about this?" he finally asked.

Niebuhr shook his head. "I checked around this morning and your name came up a couple of times, so you're the only one I called."

"Well, I'm glad people are recommending me, but why did you come to me rather than going to the police? No matter how old the case, they'd investigate a fresh lead."

"And that's all I want—just to have the possibility checked out. But Beth refuses to involve the police."

Niebuhr's tight-lipped expression told Cole how the good doctor felt about her refusal.

"And I can't go to them without her okay," he continued. "I promised her confidentiality. Besides, even if I did go—"

"Mark, you gave me your word you wouldn't tell *anyone* about this. No one except you," she added to Cole.

"And I'm not going to," Niebuhr assured her. "Discussing your...case, for lack of a better word, without your permission, would be unethical. I was merely going to say that unless you were willing to cooperate, my going to the police would be pointless."

Beth looked at Cole once more. "There's no way I can tell them that memory was of my father, because I'm not sure how much of what I remembered is real."

"You saw a very strong image," Niebuhr said.

"Mark, last night, you told me that doesn't necessarily mean it was accurate—that it was possible I'd substituted my father's face for the killer's."

"I think I said it wasn't impossible. But that doesn't make it likely."

"Well, likely or unlikely, there's no way I'm going to the police and accusing my own father of murder. Not on the basis of a memory I'm certain is...at the very least, confused."

"And I'll admit it could be," Niebuhr said. "It's even possible," he added to Cole, "that, despite the image, she didn't really see the murder at all."

Absently rubbing his jaw, Cole decided that if this

wasn't the most unusual case to ever walk into his office, it was a close second.

Beth might have witnessed the murder or she might not have. And even if she had, her memory of it could be totally wrong. There certainly wasn't a lot of *factual* information here.

"But I can't simply dismiss the possibility her memory's accurate," Niebuhr continued. "You see, she repressed it because of its incredibly strong emotional content. And if you recover such an emotion-laden memory, the odds are high that it's accurate."

"How high?"

The doctor shook his head. "When you're dealing with the workings of the human mind, quantification isn't possible."

Cole waited, but that was apparently it. "So," he said at last, "you've come to me because…?" It seemed pretty obvious, but he could hardly accept a case until somebody actually offered it to him.

"We want you to find out whether Beth's father *did* murder my wife," Niebuhr told him.

His glance flickered to Beth once more. She was clutching her hands together so tightly her knuckles were white. "Your uncle said 'we.' That's what you want, too?"

Her reply was an unhappy shrug.

"You're close to your father?"

She hesitated, then said, "We were close when I was little. But after my parents separated he moved away. Then…

"Well, he's back in Toronto now, and we *do* see each other. In fact, I'm meeting him for dinner tonight."

Cole looked at Niebuhr. The doctor shook his

head—almost imperceptibly, but it was enough to get his message across. He didn't have much doubt about the accuracy of Beth's memory, and he didn't like the idea that she'd be seeing Glen Gregory tonight.

"At any rate," she concluded, "I can't claim we're close now. There were just too many years apart. But regardless of that, and regardless of what I think I saw, my father *didn't* kill Larisa."

"If you're certain about that, why are you here?" Cole said gently.

She met his gaze again, and looking into the blue depth of her eyes, he could see how desperately she wanted to believe her father wasn't capable of murder. But he could also see a trace of doubt.

"I'm here," she said at last, "because if there's even the slightest chance he *was* the one..."

"Beth would like to see Larisa's killer identified as much as I would," Niebuhr explained. "And even though she doesn't believe her father's guilty, she's agreed to go to the police with me if you find evidence pointing in his direction. That's our compromise."

"That's *part* of our compromise," she corrected him.

Cole looked at her again. "And the other part?"

"You let me work on this with you. As an unpaid assistant."

Under different circumstances, he might have laughed. An inexperienced assistant would be more of a liability than an asset. But given the state Beth Gregory was in, she wouldn't take kindly to her proposition being laughed at.

"Sorry, but that's not an option," he told her. "I always work alone."

"Then you don't hire him," she said to her uncle. "So let's go," she added, starting to rise.

While Niebuhr gestured her back into her chair, Cole couldn't help thinking about the anemic state of his bank account. He'd had some major expenses lately, and for the past couple of months, business had been hovering between slow and stop.

Oh, there were a few things to finish up on a couple of cases, but after that he'd be straight out of work—unless he took this on.

"Look, here's the situation," Niebuhr said, shooting him a humor-the-woman glance. "Beth is understandably upset, as am I. And she's worried that a private investigator might... I'm not quite sure how to put this."

"We were told you're an ex-cop," Beth said before Niebuhr could decide on his phraseology.

"Uh-huh. The majority of private investigators probably are."

"Well, let's put what Mark was trying to say bluntly. I've heard a lot of stories about the police having tunnel vision. And if you set out trying to prove my father murdered my aunt, you might not be entirely...objective."

"I'm always objective," he said, doing his best not to let his annoyance show. But Beth Gregory had undoubtedly gotten all her police stories straight off her television set, which meant she didn't know what the hell she was talking about.

"I'm sure you're objective," Niebuhr said quickly. "And that's what both Beth and I want. Complete objectivity. We simply want to know the truth.

"Way back, Glen and I weren't only brothers-in-law, we were friends. And even though we haven't really kept in touch since he and Angela separated, I don't want to learn he murdered my wife any more than Beth does. So, hopefully, you'll find proof it wasn't him. But we have to know, one way or the other.''

''I can't guarantee I could learn anything more than you already know. Twenty-two years is a long time.''

''But you'll do your best.''

''Yes, of course. If I take the case.'' Cole glanced at Beth once more, telling himself that even though he could use the money, the last thing he wanted was a case that came with a watchdog attached. Especially one with a strong emotional involvement.

And what if her father *was* the killer? If he was, what would he do when he found out his daughter was asking questions about the murder?

The more he thought about that, the less he liked the idea of her having a damn thing to do with the investigation. So he'd better find some way to dissuade her.

''This sort of investigation could take a while,'' he explained. ''I mean, if you're intending to use vacation time...''

''No, I'm self-employed, so I can organize my time pretty much as I choose. And I'll free up as much as it takes. This is very important to me.''

''Yes, that's certainly understandable. But your working with me really isn't a good idea.''

''Look, I won't get in your way. It's just that *I* was the one who was determined to try and make the memory surface. And now... Well, I simply feel I have to see where this leads.''

"Firsthand."

"Yes, firsthand," she repeated firmly.

Cole swore to himself. Apparently, he was only going to get this job on her terms. If he didn't agree to let her tag along, she'd insist on finding somebody who would.

And he didn't like the thought of that. There were too many investigators around who were far shorter on scruples than he was, and if she got hooked up with one of them, there was no telling what kind of trouble she could find herself in.

Besides, if he went along with her idea, she'd probably get bored playing detective in no time— and that would be the end of her involvement.

"If I agree," he said, "there's no question about who calls the shots. You do what I tell you, even though you're a paying client."

"Actually, I'm the paying client," Niebuhr corrected him.

Cole nodded. The good doctor had made that clear at the outset. "Even so, she's your niece."

"Look, I've got no illusions about being Nancy Drew," Beth said quietly. "And since I don't have a clue how we should go about things, I certainly wouldn't try to call the shots."

When he didn't immediately reply to that, Niebuhr said, "There's something else you might be able to help her with."

"Oh?"

"Mark, that's nothing," Beth said. "It happens to a lot of women."

"She lives alone," Niebuhr continued, as if she hadn't spoken. "And she's been getting threatening calls."

"What kind of threatening calls?" Cole asked her.

"Just…vague threats. He says things like, 'I can get to you anytime I want, you know.' Or sometimes it isn't even a threat, but it still makes me… He'll say something like, 'I was watching you today. I like that blue suit you were wearing.'"

"And that would be on a day you *were* wearing a blue suit? I mean, he obviously *did* see you?"

She nodded.

"You don't have caller ID?"

"Yes, I do, but when he phones it reads Caller Unknown."

"Then he's probably using a cell phone. But has he ever said *why* he's watching you? Or why he might want to get to you?"

"No. I don't ask him any questions. I just hang up."

"It leaves her damn nervous, though," Niebuhr said.

"Yeah, I can see why it would."

"But that sort of thing never leads to anything more, does it?" Beth said. "I mean, crank callers are just crank callers."

"Usually," Cole told her. That wasn't always the case, though. "Do you have any idea who he is?"

"No. The voice doesn't sound quite real—more as if it's computer generated."

"He probably has some sort of voice garbler. One of the miracles of modern technology. But when did the calls start?"

"A month or so ago."

He leaned back in his chair, wondering if there could be any connection between them and her memory surfacing. A month ago, she'd already been try-

ing to remember the murder. And if the wrong person
knew that, he might not be someone who would stop
with only calls.

Looking at her again, Cole realized that if he
didn't take this case and something awful happened
to her... On the other hand, he still didn't like the
idea of having her trail along with him.

"So? What do you think?" Niebuhr said.

What he thought was that he might come to really
regret this decision. What he said was, "Well, I
guess you never know. Maybe I'll find I like having
an assistant."

Chapter Three

It was past four, Cole saw, checking his watch. He'd assumed he'd be heading home about now, but that wasn't how the afternoon had unfolded.

Leaning against the edge of his desk, he eyed Beth as she said a prolonged goodbye to her uncle. Whatever he'd expected the outcome of this appointment to be, it hadn't been that she'd stay right here so they could get started, together, immediately.

It was making him rethink the likelihood that she'd get bored and back off in short order, making him suspect he'd more likely be stuck with her for the duration. But, to be honest with himself, he might not really mind her working on a case with him—if only it wasn't this one.

She had both guts and determination, two qualities he admired. And, of course, there was also her appearance, which he couldn't help admiring, as well.

Even though he'd never had any particular weakness for blue-eyed blondes, and even though he had a rule about not mixing business with pleasure, there was something about Beth Gregory that would probably tempt him to do just that if she hung around long enough.

He told himself to stop thinking along that line and tuned into the conversation at the door.

"What about your mother?" Niebuhr was saying. "Have you decided whether you'd like me to fill her in?"

"You're sure you wouldn't mind?" Beth asked.

"No. I think she'd be a lot less upset hearing it from me. And it would certainly be easier on you."

"I guess you're right. But don't tell her too much. And don't let her even suspect I might have seen a face. Just say I've remembered a bit, and—"

"Don't worry. I'll tell her as little as possible. And I'll warn her off pumping you for details." Niebuhr gave Beth's arm a pat. "I'll stop by and see her on my way home.

"Cole?" he added, looking over. "I'd like you to call me once a day—keep me current on what's happening. I did give you a card with both my office and home number on it, didn't I?"

"Uh-huh."

"All right. Call me at either place, whenever it's convenient. And look, don't let anything happen to Beth, eh? She's the only niece I have, and I'm not entirely comfortable with all this."

"I haven't lost a client yet."

Niebuhr didn't smile. He simply turned and started down the hall.

Beth closed the door, walked back over to the visitors' chairs and picked up the briefcase she'd brought with her.

"I have photocopies of all the newspaper articles I could find about Larisa's murder," she said, sitting down and producing a file folder from the case.

That, Cole found surprising—and it made him

think she might not prove to be quite as much of a liability as he'd been assuming.

"I copied them after the nightmares started," she explained, handing him the folder. "I was hoping that reading them would jog my memory, and I thought you'd probably like to see them."

"Good idea. They should help bring me up to speed."

"Well, they're not long on detail. For some reason, the police weren't saying much to the press. But I figured they'd be a start. At any rate, is there something useful I could do while you look through them?"

When he smiled, she gave him a quizzical glance. "Did I say something funny?"

"No, you just made me wonder if you're an efficiency expert."

That made *her* smile—only fleetingly, but it was the first hint of a smile he'd seen since she'd walked into his office.

"I'm an interior designer," she said. "But I'll admit I hate wasting time."

"Good, because I was wondering if we could work through dinner."

"Sorry, but I'm meeting my father for dinner."

He nodded. "You mentioned that, and I thought maybe I could tag along. He's one of the people we'll be wanting to talk to, so we might as well start with him."

"Because you think he's guilty?" she said evenly.

"No." Which wasn't a lie. Suspecting wasn't exactly the same as thinking. But he sure didn't want her alone with her father when she dropped her little bombshell.

"I'm objective, remember?" he told her. "But I do want to see your father's reaction when you tell him we're investigating Larisa's murder. Besides, you came in your uncle's car, right? So you could use a ride."

She gazed at him for a moment. "I could go home and pick up my own car. Or take the streetcar."

He shrugged. "I'm a good man to travel with. I've got a black belt in karate. Besides, you'll like my car. It's a classic Mustang."

"You mean it's an old Mustang."

"You're obviously a hard woman to impress. But, look, I live alone, too. And I get awfully tired of my own cooking. And you hate wasting time."

"Oh...yes, okay." She pushed her hair back from her face, looking anxious. "Maybe a third person wouldn't be a bad idea, because I know I'm going to feel uncomfortable. Telling him... Well, I'm not sure exactly *how* to tell him. Or exactly *what.*

"I certainly can't say I remembered the killer having his face. That would make him feel... Lord, I can't even imagine how awful it would make him feel."

"No, you're right. You don't want to tell him that. But we'll probably be talking to a lot of people before we're finished. And every last one of them will be curious about why your uncle's hired a private investigator after all these years. And about why you're working with me. So you'll have to figure out what you want your cover story to be.

"I mean, you can't tell anyone the entire truth about what you remembered," he elaborated when she looked uncertain. "Not when you don't want the police hauling your father in for questioning."

"No...no, of course not."

"Then that's what you can do while I look at these articles. Come up with something you can say that'll sound believable."

WHEN COLE OPENED the folder and began to skim the photocopies, Beth turned her thoughts to possible cover stories and considered what options she might have—until he looked up from his reading and said, "What about this police statement that has you playing in the basement when the murder took place?"

"It's not true. I guess they were afraid the killer would come after me if he thought I might have seen him, but I was definitely in the attic. That part of my memory was always perfectly clear."

After Cole nodded and went back to the photocopies, she simply sat watching him read. She suspected there was a frustrated author living somewhere inside her, because she always found herself mentally describing people she met. But today she'd been so upset that she hadn't gotten around to doing it with him until now.

In his mid-thirties, he looked exactly like she'd have expected an ex-cop might look—one who kept in shape, at least.

He was attractive, but not in the boyishly charming way Brian was attractive. No, *boyish* definitely wouldn't describe Cole Radford. His brown hair was no-nonsense short and his features were rugged.

If she had to sum up her impression of him in one sentence, she'd probably say that he was a little rough around the edges but had a worldly-wise air about him.

If she had two sentences, she'd add that his hazel

eyes undoubtedly saw right through any bull that got slung his way. And she'd bet he didn't like people trying to tell him what to do, so she was still a little surprised he'd gone along with the idea of her working with him. But she was relieved that he had.

She knew that if Mark hadn't pressured her, she'd have simply kept on telling herself that her memory of the murder was confused—that, in reality, the killer couldn't possibly have been her father. But she owed Mark so much that when he'd insisted they either talk to the police or hire a detective, she'd given in. Very reluctantly, though.

Aside from her other misgivings, she'd had visions of ending up with some private eye straight out of a Raymond Chandler novel—one who kept a bottle of whiskey on his desk and called women "broads." Cole Radford was several cuts above that.

In fact, the man had both a fair bit of class and a reassuring manner. He'd almost convinced her he was approaching this case with an open mind—even though she knew darn well he wanted to come along to dinner because he was afraid of what might happen if her father was guilty.

She tried to ignore the chill that began creeping up her spine. Her father wasn't guilty.

Taking a deep breath, she closed her eyes and wished, yet again, she didn't have this tiny nagging fear he might be.

Finally, Cole closed the folder, put it on his desk and sat down in the chair beside hers.

The scent of his aftershave was slightly woodsy and decidedly masculine, and she liked it so much she was tempted to ask what it was. Brian had a birthday coming up.

But it was the sort of question some men would read more into than they should, and since she had no idea whether Cole was that type of man, she kept quiet.

"Okay," he said, "those articles gave me a better picture. And, luckily, I know Frank Abbot, the detective who was in charge of the investigation. He's retired now, but he's still living in Toronto, so I'll call and see if we can get together with him tomorrow."

"You think he'll see us that fast?"

"Probably. Unless he's tied up. Ex-cops love to tell war stories about their old cases."

She nodded, glad that Cole was filling her in. Maybe he hadn't wanted her working with him, but since he'd agreed to it he apparently intended to make the best of things.

"But Abbot will definitely be one of the people who'll ask why we're looking into this after all these years. So what have you come up with?"

"Well, I think for the most part I could tell people the truth. I could explain that I started having nightmares, and that I asked Mark to help me try to remember if I'd actually seen the murder or not. And maybe… What if I said I *did* finally remember seeing it? But that the killer's back was to me, so I couldn't see his face."

"No, that won't work. You *did* see his face, so—"

"No, I saw my *father's* face. And that couldn't have been right."

"Hold on. Your uncle said your memory might not be accurate. So, for the moment, let's not worry about whose face you saw."

Eyeing Cole uncertainly, she tried to decide if he

honestly believed her memory could be confused. She knew that Mark didn't. For all he was saying he simply wanted to get at the truth, he was sure he already had it. The only thing he wanted now was enough evidence to put her father behind bars.

"The point I was making," Cole continued, "was that you *did* see a face. So the killer was facing the attic door, right?"

The scene flashed into her mind once more, making her shiver.

"Yes," she said. "Larisa was the one whose back was to the stairs."

"And that would have been obvious to the crime scene investigators."

"Then…how about I say his face wasn't clear in my memory? That it was a blur. But that since I've finally remembered I did see the murder, Mark thinks talking to people about it might help me recall the details more clearly—and I might eventually be able to describe the killer."

A smile slowly spread across Cole's face. "Hey, not bad. Not bad at all. That gives us a believable reason for Mark's having hired me. You needed an experienced investigator to figure out who you should be talking to, and to kind of pave the way for you."

Beth could feel her face growing warm. A compliment was the last thing she'd expected.

"You might turn out to be Nancy Drew, after all," he added. Then his smile faded and his expression grew serious. "But look, there's something we've got to talk about before we take this any further. If the killer was somebody Larisa knew…"

"The police didn't think he was. Mark told you that—they concluded he was an unknown intruder."

"Well, what they say for public consumption isn't always true. Sometimes, they're certain who committed a crime and just don't have proof.

"At any rate, if the killer did know Larisa, and if he finds out we're asking questions... Beth, you *have* realized that by getting actively involved, you could be putting yourself in danger?"

"Well...yes," she said, although she hadn't really given the possibility much thought. She'd assumed the police *had* believed the killer was a stranger. And a stranger would have no idea what she was up to after all these years.

"I guess it's just a risk I'll have to take, isn't it?" she said, trying not to let Cole see how nervous he'd made her feel.

He shook his head. "I could talk to people on my own, without even mentioning your name— just say that some new evidence has come to light."

For a moment, she was tempted. But she'd loved Larisa. And, as Mark had said, she did want to see the killer brought to justice. And maybe, if she talked to these people in person—whoever they all turned out to be—she'd recall something important. Whereas, if she only heard things secondhand, from Cole, she might not.

So she had to be involved. She owed it to Larisa. And to Mark. And to her father. Especially to him. After all, recalling him as the killer had been nothing less than accusing him of the crime. And the only way she could make up for that was to remember the face she'd *really* seen.

"Beth?"

"I still want to play an active role," she said quietly. "I feel as if I've opened a huge can of worms, and I can't just walk away from it."

Clearly, Cole didn't like her decision. He stood up, walked over to the window, then turned and looked back at her from there.

But instead of arguing, he said, "All right, then that's the way we'll handle it. And the first thing I need is for you to tell me—in precise detail—about this image you saw last night. Tell me *exactly* what you recalled."

"Mark already told you," she said, the prospect of having to go over it, yet again, making her throat dry.

"Yes, but I need to hear it in your own words."

Actively inviting that scene to replay once more was the last thing she wanted to do. But she took a couple of slow, deep breaths, then began.

"The door at the bottom of the stairs was closed. And I could hear Larisa talking to someone. The other voice was muffled, but she was talking loudly, almost shrilly. I guess because she was terrified."

"Go on," Cole said when she paused.

Her heart began to hammer as the scene unfolded further. "I opened the door. Only enough to see a little. And just as I did... Oh, Cole, it was so awful! He started stabbing Larisa, over and over again. And..."

Her entire body froze. The colors were back, flashing crimson and white and blackish green.

"Oh, Lord," she whispered.

"What?" Cole demanded.

"Oh, Lord. I just remembered more."

As BETH'S WORDS sank in, Cole strode rapidly across his office and sat down beside her once more—hesitating for half a second, then taking her hands in his.

It might not be professional protocol, but she was ghostly white and trembling. Whatever *more* she'd remembered had obviously shaken the hell out of her.

"It's okay," he said. "You're safe."

"Yes, of course," she murmured, still looking scared to death.

He simply sat there for a minute, the scent of her perfume making him think of a spring meadow, then said, "Can you talk about it?"

"I— Just give me another few seconds. It really rattled me, but I guess it's a good thing. That more's coming back, I mean."

"I guess." He gave her hands a reassuring squeeze, then released them and sat back—very aware, once again, of how appealing he found her. She was obviously going to be the acid test of his rule about not mixing business with pleasure.

Eventually, she managed a weak smile. "I'm okay. And something else makes sense now."

He nodded for her to continue.

"Mark didn't mention this, but after I'd been having the nightmares for a while, I started having flashes."

"What do you mean?"

"I'd see sudden flashes of color—not part of the nightmares, but while I was awake. At first, they were always red and white. Then, sometimes, there'd be dark green ones.

"I was sure they had something to do with the murder, and after last night, after the memory surfaced, I knew the red ones were blood. There was blood everywhere in that hall."

Cole nodded once more. Niebuhr hadn't gone into detail, but the articles had talked about multiple stab wounds.

"There was blood everywhere," Beth repeated, as if to herself.

It made his chest feel tight. She'd been only eight years old, and a violent murder wasn't something even an adult should have to witness.

"It happened a long time ago," he said gently.

"I know. But…it must be because I never remembered before, but it seems as if it only happened yesterday. And it was…oh, Cole, it was like a horror movie. The killer would stab her, then all I'd see for an instant was a flash of red on white. But the green ones… Now I know what they were. And what the white was, too."

He waited, wishing again that he knew more about this recovered memory stuff. Maybe there were things he should be saying that would help, but he didn't have a clue.

"A garbage bag," she whispered at last. "A dark green plastic garbage bag. Larisa was lying on the floor, covered in blood. And the killer pulled a green garbage bag from the pocket of his bathrobe."

He'd been wearing a *bathrobe?* Or was this something else that might not be accurate? "Beth? Did you tell your uncle how the murderer was dressed?"

She gazed at him for a minute, then shook her head. "I only remembered that now. It was a white terry-cloth bathrobe. And it got covered in blood. Last night, all I really saw was him stabbing her. And the blood on Larisa."

And your father's face, Cole almost said. He stopped himself, though. She was having a bad enough time already.

"He took off the bathrobe," she murmured.

Cole's heart skipped a beat. "What?"

"That's what the garbage bag was for. He took off the robe and put it in the bag. The knife, as well."

"You mean you saw him standing there stark naked?"

"No, not quite. He was wearing briefs. And sneakers and socks."

"Sneakers," Cole repeated.

"I…" She shook her head. "I remember white sneakers, covered in blood. And long black socks. And then…"

"And then?" he prompted when she didn't go on.

"And then I don't know. The last thing I remember is him standing there in his underwear and sneakers, holding the garbage bag and staring down at Larisa's body."

As much as he didn't want to ask, he had to. "And in this new part you've remembered—is the killer's face clear in it?"

Beth eyed him uneasily. "Remember what you said earlier? That, for the moment, we weren't going to worry about whose face I saw?"

"You're right. And we won't."

She looked at him for another few seconds, then slowly shrugged. "Okay, yes. It was my father's again. But that only gets us back to the fact that my memory's confused."

Cole nodded. But what if it wasn't?

Chapter Four

Cole waited, not wanting to press, until Beth finally went on.

"You know, Mark told me I might gradually remember more—and that if I did, the fresh details should help correct any inaccuracies.

"And he said I should tell him, right away, if I recall anything else. But if I do, he'll ask exactly what you did. Whether it was still my father's face I saw."

"So you're thinking about not saying anything?"

She nodded. "He's already convinced my father's guilty. That must have been obvious to you. And if I add any fuel to the fire... Well, I think that, sooner or later, he *would* go to the police on his own. And if he did..."

Pausing, she gazed at Cole, her eyes filled with worry. "What if the police asked you about this case? Are you like a lawyer? Is there client privilege involved here?"

"Not exactly," he admitted.

That, he could see, made her even more worried.

"What does 'not exactly' mean?"

"It means that if the police came asking questions,

I'd do my darnedest to keep things confidential, that I wouldn't volunteer anything I figured was against my client's best interests.''

"But what if they asked you point-blank questions? Yes-or-no questions? Like whether or not I'd said it was my father's face I'd remembered seeing?''

He was tempted to lie, knowing that if he did she'd stop looking so damned anxious. But he made a point of being straight with his clients.

"I'd have to tell the truth,'' he finally said. "I'm required to cooperate with the police. I know how far I can work around that without endangering my license, but I'd never downright lie to them.

"So, look, maybe you're right. If you don't want them involved, you'd probably be smarter not to tell Mark you've recalled anything more. But there's something I want you to consider.''

"What?''

"That maybe this latest bit you've remembered means you *should* get the police involved.''

"No, I—''

"Listen to me a minute, okay? Because if that memory was accurate, I think it blows the unknown-intruder theory right out of the water.''

She caught her lower lip between her teeth, a nervous gesture that made him wish to hell he'd never agreed to her being involved in this.

At the moment, he had no way of knowing how many of the details she was recalling were accurate. But if even a fair number of them were, she could be getting in way beyond her depth by working with him. So his best move had to be convincing her of that—which meant explaining how he had things figured. Without pulling any punches.

"You remember the killer wearing a bathrobe," he said. "Do you think your garden-variety break-and-enter artist wanders around town in a bathrobe? With a garbage bag to stash the robe in if it gets bloodstained? Because he might just happen to encounter someone in a house and kill him...or her?

"Beth, if you're remembering things the way they really were, we aren't talking about a random break-in and a spur-of-the-moment murder. Someone went into your aunt's house with the intention of killing her, and took off the clothes he was wearing before he did it, so he wouldn't have to leave covered in blood.

"And if it was a planned murder, that raises the odds on this being a dangerous investigation to a whole different level."

COLE DIALED FRANK ABBOT'S number, hoping to hell the man was home. Abbot was the type who'd remember every detail about every murder case he'd investigated—which meant that the sooner they could meet with him, the better.

As the phone began to ring, he glanced over at Beth, thinking she might be the most obstinate woman he'd ever known. Any sensible person would have changed her mind about working with him the first time he'd mentioned the word *danger,* let alone when he'd told her he figured Larisa had been specifically targeted for murder.

But Beth was hanging in with bulldog tenacity, so all he could do was hope she'd soon realize she shouldn't be trying to play out of her league.

When Frank finally answered his phone, they spent a couple of minutes on social pleasantries. Then Cole got down to the purpose of the call and explained that Beth had remembered seeing the murder.

"After all this time," Frank said, a tinge of excitement in his voice.

"Yeah, amazing, eh? And since she has, Dr. Niebuhr's hired me to poke around a bit with her—see if anything we might turn up prods her memory even more. So, if you wouldn't mind talking to us, it would be a big help."

"Hell, I wouldn't mind in the least. You know how it is. The cases you don't solve keep nagging at you. And homicides are the worst for it. So sure, if you figure there's a chance of learning something new after all these years, I'll be glad to talk to you.

"The only thing is, it'll have to be either this evening or tomorrow morning. The wife and I are booked on a flight to Calgary tomorrow afternoon. One of our daughters is out there, and she's just had a baby."

"Well, hey, congratulations. And I'm sure glad I got hold of you before you left. But we're tied up tonight, so if you're not going to be pressed for time in the morning, that would be great."

"Sure, it's probably better all around. It'll give me a chance to look at my notes on the case tonight—refresh my memory."

"And you'll feel okay about sharing some of the details with us?"

"Why not? Even if the big brass found out and didn't like it, what could they do? Fire me?"

Cole laughed. "Well, I really appreciate this, because I've read some of the newspaper articles from around the time of the murder, and they're awfully light on facts.''

"Yeah…well…there were some pretty bizarre things about the case—made it one of the ones you don't want to release much information about.''

Before Cole could ask Abbot to elaborate on that, he said, "So how about you come to the house around nine-thirty? I'm on Roselawn, just west of Duplex.''

Cole jotted down the house number Abbot gave him, then thanked him and hung up.

"We're on for nine-thirty in the morning," he told Beth.

She smiled—a wan smile that said she had a whole lot more mixed feelings about working with him than she'd had earlier.

He waited, giving her a chance to say she'd reconsidered.

She didn't.

THE TRAFFIC ON KING Street West was moving at a snail's pace, and as Cole inched his Mustang along, Beth was feeling more and more uneasy.

On warm summer evenings like this, the restaurant patios sprawling out onto the sidewalk were crowded with people enjoying the late rays of sun. But at the moment, she doubted she could enjoy anything on earth.

All she seemed able to do was think about the fact that, first thing tomorrow, they'd be meeting with Frank Abbot. She was glad, of course, that he was going to help them. But actually having an appointment to see him made this situation far more real to her—and more than a little scarier.

She was almost wishing she'd given in and told Cole that yes, he *could* have the whole darned investigation to himself. That was what he'd been angling for, with his talk about how it could be a risky game she was playing. But, dammit, she wasn't playing any game, so she just couldn't worry that things might get dicey.

While they sat stuck behind a streetcar, she thought again about his suggestion that she postpone dinner with her father until after they met with Abbot. Then they'd know a lot more than they did now.

But she was still convinced she'd made the right decision. The sooner she talked to her father, the better, because… It was hard to put into words, even in her mind. But after envisioning him as the killer, she simply couldn't sit back and wait.

She wanted to tell him what was happening just as soon as possible—wanted to see his face when she told him. Or, more accurately, she wanted to see the innocence in his expression.

"We're getting to last-chance time," Cole said, glancing at her. "You're sure you want to get into this with him tonight?"

"Absolutely," she said—then immediately began wondering why she felt she had to be part of all this. Why couldn't she just let Cole do his detective thing and report back?

Probably, she decided, she needed to be involved as a way of making atonement. After all, if she'd been able to describe the murderer way back then, the police might have caught him.

Before she could come up with any other possible explanation, Cole pulled into the lot opposite the restaurant and parked. As they headed across the street, she couldn't help thinking that Rappelez-moi was *not* going to be the best place for this dinner.

One of the more popular restaurants on the King Street strip, it was usually crowded and noisy—exactly why she'd originally suggested meeting here. It had the sort of atmosphere that made the lapses in her conversations with her father less awkward. But their topic of conversation tonight called for quiet.

That was definitely not what they were going to get, she saw, spotting him. He was already seated on the tiny sidewalk patio where the tables were even closer together than the ones inside.

"That's him. The man in the dark suit," she said, trying to see him through Cole's eyes.

There was nothing particularly out of the ordinary about him. Like Mark, he had regular features, was average height and hadn't put on many extra pounds over the years.

His brown hair had gone gray around the temples, making him very distinguished looking. Even so, he wasn't quite as elegant as her uncle—didn't worry about whether his suits were perfectly tailored or his hair was precisely the right length. Still, nobody would have trouble believing he was a successful financial planner.

He rose to greet her as she neared the table, glancing curiously at Cole. He wasn't too crazy about Brian, so he was probably hoping Brian was out and Cole was in. But when he heard what the *real* story was...

A waiter appeared with an extra chair while she introduced her father to Cole—without explaining who he was. She wasn't quite ready to get into that yet. Actually, given the way her stomach was doing flip-flops, she might not be ready by the time dessert arrived.

She eyed the beer in front of her father, wondering if she should order a double of something. Or even a triple. But since she wasn't much of a drinker, she simply went with a glass of chardonnay.

By the time that arrived, along with the beer Cole had ordered, they'd worked their way through the topic of the weather and how pleasant it was on the patio.

"So, what's new in your life?" her father asked when the waiter turned away. He didn't even glance in Cole's direction as he delivered the line, but she knew he meant, *So who is this and why is he having dinner with us?*

"Well," she said nervously, "there *is* something new. So new, in fact, that you're the first person I'm telling about it—aside from Cole here and Mark. Dad...I've begun to recall things about Larisa's murder."

"Really?" he said slowly.

She nodded without breaking eye contact. "I started having nightmares about it. And they were bothering me so much I was ready to try anything to make them stop. So I asked Mark to help me out. And it took a while, but just last night I remembered seeing what happened."

"Oh, Beth," he murmured. "That must have been terribly upsetting."

His concern was so obviously for her, not about what she'd remembered seeing, that a sense of relief spread through her. But it was relief mixed with guilt.

She'd known he wasn't the killer. So regardless of

that image, how could she have had even the slightest doubt?

"And you've got something to do with this?" he asked Cole.

"Only after the fact." He looked at Beth. "Do you want to explain the rest, or shall I?"

"Why don't you," she said, hating the thought that flashed through her mind.

It would be easier to concentrate on her father's reactions with Cole doing the explaining. But if she was totally convinced of his innocence, why should she care about watching them?

Cole took a card from his wallet and handed it to Glen Gregory. "I'm a private investigator," he said, watching the man's face as he spoke. "Now that Beth's remembered a little, Mark Niebuhr has hired me to see if I can turn up any clues to the murderer's identity."

Gregory eyed the card for a moment, then looked at Beth. "You know, all I was thinking was how dreadful it must have been to remember seeing the murder. I didn't even think about the fact that you'd have remembered seeing the murderer, too."

She merely nodded, but Cole could sense her anxiety. Her father looked and sounded like innocence personified. If he were the killer, though, innocence was exactly what he'd be trying to project.

"Did you recall what you saw very clearly?" he asked. "After so long a time?"

Beth slowly shook her head. "No, nothing was very clear, especially not what the killer looked like. But I'm going to tag along with Cole while he's talking to people about the case. Mark thinks there's a chance that something I hear might bring back more details.''

Still keeping a surreptitious eye on Gregory, Cole sat back and took a sip of his beer. Even though they'd gone over what she should say, he'd been worried that she'd tell her father she was already beginning to remember specific details—if for no other reason than to demonstrate her trust in him. And if he proved the wrong man to trust...

''You don't think tagging along might be awfully hard on you?'' he said to Beth. ''I know it's been a long time, but you adored Larisa. So digging around about her murder, talking to people about it—Beth, if you remember more details, if your memory becomes more clear, it could be very tough to deal with.''

''I realize that, but I feel it's something I have to do.''

''I see. Well, this all certainly comes as a shock.'' Gregory turned to Cole. ''But does Mark really think that an investigation is going to do any good? I don't mean that as an insult, but even if Beth remembers more, can you realistically expect to turn up anything new after twenty-two years?''

''It's possible.''

''Yes, I guess anything's possible.'' Gregory focused on his daughter again. ''You said I'm the first person you've told. That includes your mother?''

Beth nodded. ''Although I imagine she knows by now. Mark was going to drop by and fill her in. He said it would probably be better all around if he did it. I guess I was being a chicken, but I took him up on the offer.

''My mother's going to be upset,'' she added to

Cole. "She's always thought it was a blessing I'd blocked out that hour."

"I remember she used to say she wished she could have blocked it out," Gregory said. "Or, at least, the part of it she was there for. As best we can figure, she got there shortly after the killer left. But she went into shock when she found the body, and it was a while before she pulled herself together enough to phone the police."

Beth nodded. "She still hasn't gotten over it, you know. Even after all these years, she can't bear to talk about it."

The waiter had arrived to take their dinner orders, and as Beth gave him hers, Cole considered that last statement.

Since Angela Gregory had been the one who'd discovered the body, it was hardly surprising that she'd have been traumatized. But after twenty-two years she still couldn't talk about it? That seemed extreme. Unless she'd done more than just find the body.

He mentally shook his head. Ninety-nine percent of the time, he was a logical thinker. It was essential in his line of work. Yet, every now and then, a completely crazy idea popped into his head—and this one really took the cake.

He told himself to stop imagining the absurd. But Niebuhr had referred to Angela Gregory as "erratic," which might have been his way of saying she was a little unbalanced.

And one of those newspaper articles had called the victim "diminutive"—which meant Larisa hadn't been someone only a strong man could have stabbed to death.

Of course, it was a *man* Beth recalled.

On the other hand, she kept insisting her memory was confused. And Niebuhr had said…

Cole tried to remember the psychiatrist's exact words. They'd been something like, "We're talking about a memory she repressed because of its incredibly strong emotional content."

And hell, how much stronger emotional content could there be than seeing your mother kill her own sister?

IT WAS TWILIGHT by the time Cole and Beth left Rappelez-moi and said goodbye to Glen Gregory.

His silver BMW was parked on the street, practically in front of the restaurant, and several passersby watched him getting into it. Gregory seemed oblivious to the stares, or maybe he was simply used to them. The sleek lines of an M3 coupe probably attracted a lot of attention.

Cole watched it pull away, wondering if Gregory had glanced back at them. With the side and back windows darkly tinted, it was almost impossible to see the driver, let alone tell what he was doing.

"Well?" Beth said as the car disappeared into the flow of traffic. "Now that you've met him, you see why I was insisting he couldn't have done it?"

"Uh-huh."

She smiled, looking relieved, so Cole didn't say anything more while they walked to his car. But his seeing why she'd insist her father wasn't a murderer didn't make it a fact. Killers came in all shapes and sizes.

When that thought started him wondering about Angela Gregory again, he told himself to stop. It was

Beth's father who was the likely suspect. And the fact he seemed like a nice-enough guy hardly guaranteed he wasn't harboring deep, dark secrets.

Pulling out of the parking lot, Cole headed west on King, toward the old factory district where Beth had said her apartment was.

She seemed content to simply gaze out the window, so he let himself think about Glen Gregory some more. When she'd told him about her recovered memory, his only overt reaction had been fatherly concern.

Still, the fact remained it was *his* face she'd remembered. Which had been enough to convince Mark Niebuhr that Gregory was the killer. And a psychiatrist knew a hell of a lot more about recovered memories than a private investigator—than this one, at least.

But how much faith could you really put in a memory that had surfaced after twenty-two years? One that Beth, herself, insisted was confused?

"You want to turn left at the next corner," she said.

He flicked on his signal and turned.

"Then it's a right and a quick left onto my street—Wilson Place."

Wilson Place, which he'd never even heard of before, proved to consist of a single block tucked in between Wellington and Front. It was a mix of small factories—some that appeared to be still operational, others that looked as if they'd shut down long ago, and a few buildings that had been converted into residential units.

"It's the sandblasted one up on the right," Beth said.

He pulled over to the curb and surveyed it. A typical old brick warehouse, four stories high with a flat roof, it had probably gone residential during the early eighties, when renovators were spending big bucks on features like this building's expanse of dark marble framing the front entrance, the ornate carriage lights and the brass handrails running up the sides of the steps.

"Originally, there were plans to turn the entire street residential. But that was before the real estate market went bust," Beth told him. "Well, I'll see you in the morning. You're sure you want to pick me up, though? I could easily meet you at Frank Abbot's."

"No, it makes more sense to go together."

"Okay, then I'll be ready at nine."

When she opened her door, he opened his as well. "I'll walk you to the entrance. It's pretty deserted around here." Definitely not the safest place for a woman to live on her own, he silently added.

"It isn't the ideal location," she said, as if she'd read his thought. "But the apartments are great. And I work out of mine, so being on the fringe of downtown is handy for clients. Besides, if I'm coming home alone at night I'm usually in my car."

"And you park it...?"

He glanced along the block. The streetlight in front of her building was burned out, and the moon was casting strange shadows. Without even trying, he could pinpoint a dozen places where someone might be hiding.

"There's an underground garage."

"In an old building like this?"

She shrugged. "The renovators were magicians.

The entrance is just down that drive on the far side of the building. It's a safe garage,'' she added, at his quizzical glance. "Well lit."

"That helps," he said as they crossed the sidewalk. But if she believed that made it safe, she shouldn't be let out at night without a keeper.

They walked up the front steps and stopped at the door.

"I'm fine from here, assuming I can find my keys," she said, digging through her purse. "Unless you'd like coffee?"

He almost said yes. Surprisingly, given the circumstances, he'd enjoyed being with her tonight.

But she was a client, not a date, so he shook his head. "Thanks, but coffee and I don't get along this late."

"I have decaf."

On the other hand, if he went in, they could discuss exactly how they were going to approach Frank Abbot in the morning. He'd been planning to do that on the way to the man's house, but maybe tonight would be better.

Just as her smile was making him decide it would, a gunshot exploded.

Chapter Five

Beth started at the noise.

Then Cole was diving at her, propelling her so roughly down the stairs and into the sheltered space beside them that her ankle twisted.

It wasn't until the second blast, until she heard a brick splinter in the wall above her, that it dawned on her the earsplitting sounds were gunfire. With the realization, her heart began hammering even faster. But after the first two shots, there was only silence.

They stayed right where they were, Cole's body pressing her so hard into the building that she could scarcely breathe. But where was the shooter?

She couldn't keep from imagining him stalking down the street toward them, couldn't stop thinking that any second he'd be firing again—from point-blank range.

"Don't you have any curious neighbors?" Cole whispered at last. "Why hasn't anyone come out?"

"They must have figured it was just a car back-firing," she whispered back. "That's what I thought at first."

"Well, you've got shards of brick in your hair to

prove it wasn't. Don't move," he added, easing away.

Cautiously, he half stood and peered along the street. "Okay, it looks clear. But stay where you are, just in case. My phone's in the car, and I've got to call the cops right now. Otherwise there won't be even a chance of them spotting him."

He was halfway across the sidewalk before it occurred to her that her phone was in her purse, that he could have used it. Then she discovered she didn't have her purse. She must have dropped it somewhere between the front door and the shelter of the stairs.

Still crouched down, and trying to ignore the way her ankle was aching, she edged forward so she could see more.

Cole was sitting in the car, his phone to his ear. The street was as quiet and lifeless as it normally was at this time of night. But the sounds of the shots were still ringing in her ears, and terrifying thoughts were scurrying around in her brain.

Had the shooter merely been some loony on the loose? Or had he known exactly who he was shooting at? Had he been waiting here, on her street, for her to arrive home?

Trying to ignore the chill slithering up her spine, she told herself not to jump to conclusions. She'd wait and see what Cole thought. He was the ex-cop here.

Finally, he climbed out of the car and headed back across the sidewalk, pausing only to retrieve her purse from the steps.

"You don't think our friend will come back, do you?" she asked.

"I almost wish he would. I don't normally carry

my gun, but I was at the shooting range this morning and it was still in the glove compartment. I've got it on me now.''

That must mean Cole figured there was a chance the shooter would be back, she thought nervously. And why would he figure that unless he thought it hadn't been just a random shooting?

"Let's get inside." He offered his hand to help her up.

"What about the police? Will they be coming?"

"Uh-uh. I got around that by talking to an officer I know. We don't want to be sitting here at midnight with a couple of cops. Not when I just told my buddy all there is to tell.''

Letting go of Cole's hand, she tentatively put a little weight on her ankle. It didn't feel too bad, but her first step made her breathe in sharply with pain.

"What's wrong?" he demanded.

"Nothing serious. I just twisted my ankle.''

"Damn, that was my fault, wasn't it. My take-cover routine needs work.''

"Don't worry about it. At least I'm not dead.''

"Yeah." He gave her a grim smile. "Yeah, I guess it's all in the way you look at it. But put your weight on me so you don't make things any worse.'' With that, he wrapped his arm around her waist and helped her hobble up the stairs.

After the front door had closed behind them, she started feeling better. Not much, though. She'd never been shot at before, and it wasn't something she ever wanted to experience again.

But once they were standing waiting for the elevator, Cole's arm still firmly around her, she began to calm down considerably. After all, the shooter was probably miles away by now. Of course, if he was, there'd be almost no chance of the police picking him up.

When she voiced that thought, Cole said, "They might find him. I got a quick look at him—saw enough that I was able to give them a description. But let's wait and talk about things when we get upstairs."

She nodded. Waiting until she'd recovered a little more was probably a good idea.

"You're sure you're okay?" he added, glancing down at her as he spoke.

She could feel the warmth of his breath fanning her skin, and the sensation sent a tiny ripple of desire through her. In one way, it took her completely by surprise. Only minutes ago they'd almost been killed, and it seemed bizarre that she was aware of being attracted to any man when she'd barely stopped shaking.

On the other hand, it was Cole who'd rescued her from the line of fire. So why should feeling something positive toward him be even remotely surprising?

After considering that for a moment, she silently admitted she was trying to fool herself. There was a big difference between "something positive" and what she'd just felt.

But she didn't want to start feeling that way about him. Or to be so aware, this very minute, of the way the heat from his body was mingling with her own body heat. And if she didn't want to be feeling these things, then she shouldn't be standing with her body pressed against his.

"My ankle's starting to feel better," she said. "I think I'll be able to walk all right now."

"Good."

When he took his arm from around her, she told herself she'd just made a very wise move. She had Brian in her life. She wasn't in the market for any other man. And she certainly didn't need any unnecessary complications while she was working with Cole.

She glanced at him and caught him watching her, as if he knew exactly what she was thinking. And since that was the last thing she wanted him to know, she mentally scrambled for something to say. Anything, as long as it would make him figure she hadn't been thinking about him.

"This elevator," she finally said, gesturing toward its brass door. An elevator might be a pretty inane topic of conversation, but it was the best she could come up with.

"It was once the private elevator to a suite in an elegant old hotel. The people who renovated here bought it when the hotel was being demolished."

"Aah," he said, looking as if he wondered why on earth she was telling him the history of an elevator.

Fortunately, before she could say anything even more improbable, the brass door slid open.

"What do people do on moving day?" he asked when he saw how small the interior was.

"Oh, there's a freight elevator in the back of the building, left over from its warehouse days. And it's huge."

Inside the tiny confines of this one, though, there was no choice about standing only inches away from

Cole. And like it or not, she was feeling very aware of him again.

Telling herself it was something she'd just have to ignore, she tried to do exactly that until they reached her floor.

"Everything look okay?" he said when the door opened and they started down the hall.

The question made her uneasy. "Why wouldn't it?"

He shrugged. "Standard question. I'm a detective, remember?"

She stopped in front of her door, caught his gaze and held it. Downstairs, he'd suggested waiting to talk about things until they got up here. Now something in his eyes was telling her there were more "things" than she was aware of.

"Let's get inside where you can take your weight off that ankle."

"All right," she said slowly. Until he got around to telling her exactly what was bothering him, she simply wouldn't let herself wonder about it. Her imagination would probably come up with some pretty horrible possibilities.

"This leads into my office," she said, inserting the key. "I'd like to have a second door, directly into the apartment area, but the owners won't go for the idea."

"Landlords are like that, aren't they?"

She managed a smile, but she didn't like this game of pretending nothing was wrong when she knew there was. Opening the door, she flicked on the light—just a little nervously.

When her office looked perfectly normal, she felt a flutter of relief. Then Bogey and Bacall came meowing hungrily in from the apartment, the way they always did when she got home late.

While she bent to stroke them, she kept one eye on Cole. He was glancing around at the gray suede-covered office walls, the Spartan-straight raw-silk drapes, and the enormous Louis XVI bookcase that held both books and her collection of glass paperweights.

"I'm impressed," he said, his gaze lingering on her mahogany partners desk.

Forcing another smile, she stood up, wincing when pain shot through her ankle. "Good. An interior designer's office is an advertisement for her work."

"And these guys are...?" he asked, gesturing at the cats who were now wrapping themselves around her legs.

"Actually, only Bogey's a guy. Bacall's a female. But since they're both fixed, it probably doesn't matter."

"Oh, I'll bet it matters to a guy named Bogey—fixed or not. He's got a macho image to live up to."

"Well, he doesn't do a very good job of it. He's a real sweetie."

She led the way through to the apartment, trying not to limp. But she obviously wasn't successful, because when she started for the kitchen, Cole said, "Will you just sit down before you make that really bad?"

"As soon as I feed the cats."

"I'll feed them. You sit."

"Well...okay. Thanks. The cans are in the cupboard to the right of the sink. And Bogey's bowl is the blue one, Bacall's is the pink."

Cole shot her a wry glance.

"I know," she said before he could say anything. "It's awfully stereotypical, but I wasn't in a feminist mood the day I bought them."

"What I was going to say was that I'm still missing information. I don't know which cat is which."

"Oh, sorry. The gray one's Bogey and the rusty one's—"

"Bacall." Cole smiled. "I don't need it entirely spelled out."

"No, of course not. You're a detective," she said, surprised to find she was up to saying anything even remotely humorous.

"Very funny," he muttered, but then he smiled again.

He had, she thought as she headed for the couch, a very engaging smile.

The message light on her answering machine was flashing, so she pressed it while she eased off her shoes, certain she knew who'd called.

She was right.

"Beth," her mother's worried voice said, "Mark just left, and I'm terribly concerned about you. Why didn't you tell me you were having sessions with him? And now you're going to be traipsing around with a private eye?

"I just...well, I guess, at this stage, there's no point in saying I don't think forcing yourself to remember was a good idea. But if you're feeling even the least bit fragile, I want you to come home and stay at the house for a while.

"I'm going to be out tonight—possibly quite late—but you know where the spare key's hidden. And if you don't come, be sure to call me in the morning. I want to talk to you about working with this private eye."

Pushing Rewind, Beth glanced over at Cole.

"She leaves a spare key hidden?" he said. "Doesn't she know what a bad idea that is?"

"Well, she has a problem with losing her keys. Actually, I do, too. I think it's genetic."

"But you don't have one hidden out in the hall, do you?"

"No, my solution's to carry an extra set. But my mother figures she's got a hiding place that nobody would ever find."

"Which means it's not under the mat or in the mailbox. But let me guess. Under a rock in the garden?"

Beth smiled. "You got it in one. Still, it would take someone a while to turn over every rock in the garden."

"There are crooks who leave no stone unturned," he said dryly.

When that made her smile again, he grinned. "Two smiles in a row? I think I'll quit while I'm ahead." With that, he went back to dishing out the cat food.

Watching him across the counter that separated the kitchen from the living area, she was surprised that such a ruggedly masculine man could look so domesticated. "Do you have a cat?" she asked when he looked over again.

"Not anymore. When my marriage broke up, my ex wife got custody."

So that was why he lived alone. She was tempted to ask why his marriage had broken up. And about whether there were any children his ex-wife had gotten custody of, as well. But since she intended to keep things strictly business between them, asking anything more about his personal life wouldn't be a good idea.

When he put the bowls back down on their mat, the cats gave him a couple of grateful meows before digging in.

He headed over to the couch, reaching beneath the back of his jacket as he walked and producing a handgun. "This won't make you nervous if I put it on the coffee table, will it?"

She shook her head, although it actually did make her nervous. But in another way it made her feel safer.

"So," he said, kneeling down. "Let me have a look at that ankle."

"Oh, no, don't bother. I'm sure it's fine."

Ignoring her words, he gingerly took her foot in his hands.

She swallowed hard. She'd never thought of her foot as an erogenous zone, but when he began moving his fingers slowly over it, she felt a lazy, sensual warmth spreading through her.

"A little swollen," he murmured. "Does this hurt?" He gently twisted her ankle.

"Only a bit."

"Good. I think, at worst, it's a minor sprain. Maybe not even that bad. But if it's bothering you in the morning, you should put on a tensor bandage. I—" He stopped speaking as the phone began to ring.

"I'll let the machine pick up," she said, glancing anxiously over at it.

"If it's your crank caller, let me pick up."

They waited, Beth hoping it was her crank. But it was Brian's voice that finally came on the machine. "Beth, are you there, love?"

She looked at Cole, the strangest feeling in her chest. Then it vanished before she could identify it.

"Excuse me," she said, forcing her eyes from his. "I'd better take this."

COLE HAD BEEN TRYING not to listen in on Beth's conversation, but hadn't been doing a very good job of it.

So far, he'd gathered her caller's name was Brian, that he was some kind of troubleshooter for a computer company, and that the company was having major problems out West—which meant that Brian had a suddenly scheduled trip to Vancouver in the morning.

Beth, for her part, was giving him little information. She hadn't even mentioned the shooting. Mostly, she'd just been making the occasional comment in response to things he said.

"So you don't know how long you'll be gone?" she asked.

During the silence following that, Cole focused on one of the paintings. It was done in warm shades of yellow and orange and seemed perfect in the room. Of course, everything seemed perfect in the room.

The two pale rugs that defined the living and dining areas were nubby wool, so thick his shoes sank into them.

The couch and chairs were big and comfortably stuffed, yet elegant. And even though they were contemporary, they looked just right with the antique accents and the big old polished armoire that he assumed concealed a television and CD player and whatever. The dining room furniture was also antique, although he had no idea what style it was.

He also had no idea how all those centuries-old pieces could look as if they'd been made for this modern space, with its clean lines, snowy white walls and skylights.

Somehow, Beth had pulled everything together so the apartment seemed eminently lived-in, yet looked like a picture from a glossy magazine. From what he'd seen so far, she was a first-rate designer.

Looking at her, he found himself wondering if her career was the most important thing in her life. And if that explained why she wasn't married. But what did it matter to him?

Nothing, he told himself.

"Brian, it's all right," she said, breaking the silence. "When you figure out what's happening, you can let me know."

Bogey wandered over and began purring at Cole's feet, so he picked up the little guy and scratched him behind the ear, forcing his thoughts back to that incident in the street.

It might have been just a random shooting, of course, but his gut was telling him it hadn't been. There were reasons this city was known as Toronto the Good. And one of them was that there weren't many random shootings.

"Me, too," Beth said into the phone, so quietly he barely heard the words.

He rubbed the cat under its chin. "Me, too," as in she'd miss this Brian? Or "me, too," as in she loved him?

Obviously, she was seriously involved with the

guy. Which meant that Mr. Cole Radford had better just forget about those thoughts that had been sneaking around in his head. The ones telling him there were exceptions to every rule—including his one about not mixing business and pleasure.

From here on in, he was going to ignore the fact she was an attractive woman. And ignore the way her scent made him think of a meadow in spring.

He'd also stop noticing that whenever she wasn't too anxious or frightened, a neat sense of humor surfaced. From here on in, she was a client. Period.

While Brian was saying a prolonged goodbye, Beth kept guiltily thinking she still had time to tell him about what had been happening since she'd last seen him.

But she just didn't feel it would be a good idea. Given that he hadn't approved of her trying to remember Larisa's murder, learning she had wasn't going to make him happy. So it was something that would be better discussed in person.

As for her getting shot at... Well, telling him about that would only make him worry while he was away, and he already worried about her too much. It would also give him more ammunition for his ongoing argument that they should be living together.

That, she thought fleetingly, was something she'd have to make a decision about soon. He hadn't exactly given her an ultimatum, but it was obvious that he'd almost run out of patience.

As if she were sending thought vibes through the phone lines, he said, "So, while I'm away, think some more on what we've been talking about, eh? You know how much I worry about you living in that neighborhood alone."

"I know," she murmured. But until she was sure she loved him enough to take things a stage further...

"I'll call you once I see what's what. You take care while I'm gone, eh?"

"Of course I will. You, too. Bye."

Hanging up, she looked across the coffee table to where Cole was sitting. "Sorry that took so long."

"No problem."

"What about the decaf? Would you like me to make some?"

He shook his head. "Thanks, but I just want to talk to you for a minute and then I'll head home."

"All right," she said slowly. Finally, they were getting to whatever it was he'd been holding off saying, and his expression told her she wasn't going to like hearing it.

"Beth, I'm afraid there's no way of putting this without frightening you, but try not to let it scare you too much."

"All right," she said again, mentally bracing for the worst.

"I think we've got to assume that guy with the gun was specifically after you."

"Oh, Lord," she whispered. Even though she'd already realized that might be the case, hearing Cole say he thought it was made things seem far worse.

"He might not have been, but it would be dangerous as hell for us not to proceed as if he was."

When she tried to speak, her throat was so dry that she had to swallow a couple of times before she could. "That's why you asked if everything looked okay when we first got up here, isn't it," she said at last. "You think if it was someone trying to kill me, he might try again. And that he might come right into the building to do it.''

Cole pushed himself out of his chair and walked over to the couch. "Look," he said, sitting down beside her. "When I phoned the police, I left my cell phone number. If they pick up the guy, they'll call me. Then we'll know you'll be safe."

"They won't pick him up," she said, trying to get control of her fear. "On a nice night like this, there must be thousands of men wandering around out there."

"Not wearing coveralls."

"Coveralls," she repeated.

Cole nodded. "Like garage mechanics wear. And he had on a gorilla mask. One of those rubber jobs you pull on over your head."

She could feel her fear escalating. "A mask. But he'd have taken that off right away, wouldn't he? As soon as he was out of sight?"

"Probably. Still, a guy wearing coveralls... The police might spot him."

"Why didn't you tell me about the mask? Before now?"

"You were already frightened, so I figured it could wait."

"But it means he *was* specifically after me, doesn't it? That there's no doubt about it. I was thinking he might just have been some loony. But if he was wearing a mask, it was so that if he missed me I wouldn't be able to identify him."

"That's not necessarily why he was wearing one. Maybe he *was* just some loony. After all, it hasn't cooled off much yet. So would a sane man be walking around in coveralls and a rubber mask?"

She shook her head, aware Cole was trying to lighten things up but unable to manage a smile.

"Look, Beth," he said quietly. "Unless they get the guy, we won't be sure if he was specifically after you or not."

"I guess we won't," she said slowly. But she knew Cole was almost certain he had been—that somewhere out in the night was a man who wanted to kill her.

The thought was still lingering in her mind, refusing to leave, when Cole's cell phone rang. Anxiously, she watched him take it out of his pocket and answer it.

"No," he said after listening for a minute. "No, odds were you wouldn't. But thanks for letting me know.

"They didn't spot him," he said, clicking the phone off and putting it on the coffee table next to his gun.

Even though she hadn't thought they *would* spot him, the news started her stomach churning. "What now?" she said.

"Well, now we hope the loony theory's the right one, and that he's long gone. But we can't take any chances. So tell me about this building. I want to be sure you're safe here."

She nodded. She'd tell him about whatever he wanted, because as long as they were talking, he'd still be here—and she wouldn't be left alone with her fear.

Besides, while she was talking about the building, she wouldn't be thinking about the shooter. And he was something she really didn't want to think about.

"There are only two apartments on each floor,"

she began. "The ones like mine, that run across the front of the building, and mirror-image ones that run across the back."

"And what about that window I noticed at the end of the hall? Is there a fire escape off it?"

"Yes."

"Could someone easily get onto it from street level?"

"No...not easily." But with a ladder it wouldn't be any challenge. That realization was very unsettling. And it blew the theory that she wouldn't think about the shooter while she was talking.

When Cole glanced up at the skylights, she nervously followed his gaze. Once, she'd looked up and a cat had been staring down at her, and that had almost made her jump out of her skin. So what if...?

She gazed over to where her own cats were curled up together in a chair, fast asleep in the safety of their home. But what if her apartment *wasn't* safe?

The thought it might not be made her want to run and hide. Only where could she run?

Not to her mother's house. As much as she loved her mother, she couldn't face the thought of being hovered over as if she were still a child. And even if she did try to hide, whom would she be hiding from? Who wanted to kill her? And why?

A couple of possible answers came to mind, and she didn't like either of them.

"Cole?"

He looked at her, the concern in his eyes making her even more worried.

"If that man was specifically after me... Why do you think he would be?"

"Well," he said slowly, "it could be that your

crank caller isn't the type who stops with threats. Or it might have something to do with your remembering Larisa's murder.''

Closing her eyes, she exhaled slowly. Those had been the possibilities she'd thought of, too, and she didn't know which of them scared her more.

Chapter Six

Beth was looking so darned upset again that Cole said, "Hey, I didn't mean the guy *couldn't* have been just someone wandering around looking for a moving target. I only said we don't want to take any chances. And remember what I told your uncle? I've never lost a client."

She made a dismal attempt at a smile.

"Look, you're going to be all right. I promise." He rested his hand on hers, but when the soft warmth of her skin started a slow heat curling in his loins, he rose and walked over to the living room window.

Gazing out into the darkness, he tried to visualize that guy in his coveralls and mask. As he did, his off-the-wall suspicion about Beth's mother began nagging at him again.

Her message on the answering machine had said she'd be out tonight. And, dammit, he hadn't gotten a really good look at the shooter, so how could he be certain their man hadn't actually been a woman?

He turned away from the window and watched Beth, resisting the temptation to ask if her mother was tall. In the morning, when they were talking to

Frank Abbot, he'd find out whether the cops had been certain Larisa's murderer was a man.

In the meantime, he'd be better off thinking along other lines, because the odds on Angela Gregory having killed her own sister had to be one in a million. And the odds against a woman trying to kill her own daughter had to be higher still.

Finally, Beth looked over at him. "The more I think about it, the less I can believe there'd be any connection between me remembering Larisa's murder and getting shot at. The only people who know I've remembered are you and Mark."

"And your parents."

She slowly shook her head. "I thought meeting my father had convinced you he wasn't a killer."

When he wandered back and sat down beside her again, simply letting the remark pass, she said, "We came here straight from the restaurant. So unless you figure my father had a gun, coveralls and a gorilla mask in the trunk of his car, he wasn't out in the street shooting at us."

"Yeah, you're right." And her father hadn't struck him as the type to be driving around with a disguise in his trunk. But almost anything was possible.

"I guess what's really bothering me," he said at last, "is that two very unusual things have happened to you within the past twenty-four hours. Last night you remembered seeing the murder. Tonight you got shot at. So it just seems logical that the two might be related."

"There are such things as coincidences."

"Sure there are. But a coincidence like this one sets off alarms in my brain."

Beth clearly didn't want to hear what he was saying, but he had to keep going. It was better for her to be scared than dead.

"Look, I hope I'm completely off base here, and that guy with the mask didn't have a clue who you were. But just let me think out loud for a minute. You haven't told anyone else that you've remembered, right? Nobody except your uncle. And then your father."

"Right."

"Okay. Your father wouldn't have had time to mention it to anyone before the shooting. But what about your uncle? Would he have said anything?"

"No, it wouldn't be ethical. You heard him say that yourself."

"But he did tell your mother. And he was on his way to her place when he left us. So she's known about it for hours. Phone and ask if she's told anyone."

"Her message said she'd be out late."

"It said *possibly* she would, so try her."

Beth reached for the cordless and punched in a number. "Her machine's picked up," she said after a minute.

"Make sure she's not just screening the call."

"Mom?" she said after another few seconds. "Mom, are you there?" She waited, then added, "You're not home yet. Well, it's all right. I didn't want anything important, so don't worry. I'll call you tomorrow."

"Okay," he said as she put down the phone. "Did anyone other than Mark know you were even trying to remember?"

"Only a couple of friends."

"Who?"

"My best friend, whose name is Wendy Kinahan, and a fellow I'm...seeing. Brian Robertson."

So that was how she defined her relationship with the guy who'd phoned. She was "seeing" him.

Cole didn't know exactly what that amounted to in her book, but from what he'd overheard, things were obviously pretty serious between them.

Reminding himself that was no concern of his, he said, "When did you tell them about it?"

"A while before I began the sessions with Mark. After the nightmares started, I told them about photocopying the articles—about how I was hoping they'd help me remember. And hoping that, if I did, the nightmares would stop."

"Then, at this point," Cole said slowly, "we really have no idea who might know."

"What do you mean?"

He shrugged. "It's an interesting story—someone trying to remember witnessing a long-ago murder—so I'd be surprised if both Wendy and Brian didn't mention it to a few people. Then, whoever they told would have repeated it, until pretty soon a whole lot of people would have known about it. And if one of them didn't want you to recall what you saw..."

"You're saying Larisa's killer might have learned I was trying to remember? Oh, Cole, there are coincidences and then there are coincidences."

"Well..." He hesitated, but now that he'd gone that far there was no point to stopping. "Let's get back to the idea that the unknown-intruder theory was wrong. If Larisa's killer knew her, then he'd know who you are. And it wouldn't have been impossible to keep tabs on you over the years."

"Because he was afraid I'd someday remember seeing him?"

"Exactly. Even if he believed the police statement that said you were playing in the basement, he'd know there was a chance you saw him coming or going."

Beth closed her eyes, telling herself Cole was way off base. After all, the police had spent months investigating the murder, while he'd done nothing more than read those articles and ask her and Mark a few questions. So surely the police had been right.

Then she remembered why he figured the unknown-intruder theory was wrong. It was because of what she'd recalled only this afternoon. She'd never told the police about the killer wearing a bathrobe, then taking it off and putting it into the garbage bag. She'd never told anyone except Cole. So maybe he wasn't off base at all. Maybe she *was* being stalked by the killer.

The thought was so frightening it made her throat tight.

"Beth?" Cole said quietly. "The murderer might be long dead. Or living thousands of miles from Toronto. I didn't want to scare you half to death. I just want you to realize you have to be very careful."

She simply nodded, afraid if she tried to speak she'd end up crying. She felt as if she'd made the biggest mistake of her life by forcing that memory to surface. And she had a horrible sense she'd only be compounding her mistake if she pushed things any further.

Taking a deep breath, she made her decision. "Cole, I'm having second thoughts about working with you. I think my father was right, that I'd find talking to people about the murder awfully difficult. So it would be better if I just left everything up to you."

"I see," he said, thinking rapidly. Only hours ago he hadn't wanted her working with him. Now he was afraid to let her out of his sight.

"I should have given it more thought in the first place," she continued. "But since you didn't really want me tagging along, anyway, I guess it's just as well I've changed my mind."

"Look...I'll tell you what."

"What?"

"Go with me to see Frank Abbot in the morning, the way we planned. If you start finding the discussion too upsetting, you can wait for me in the car. And if you don't want to talk to anyone else after that, I won't ask you to.

"It's important," he added, when he saw she didn't want to go along with the idea.

"Why?"

"We need to find out if there was evidence suggesting the killer knew Larisa. And even if there wasn't, I want you to tell Abbot about the details you've remembered—see what he makes of them."

"You could tell him."

"It would be better if you did."

She shook her head. "You said you could easily talk to people without my being involved. And after tonight I'll feel a lot safer if I'm not."

He exhaled slowly, at a complete loss as to where he went from here. He could hardly drag her around with him against her will.

"What?" she said quietly. "There's something you aren't telling me."

"I..."

"What?"

"We'll be able to assess things a lot better after we've talked with Abbot. Until then...well, I've just got a horrible feeling you might already be too involved to back off. And until we know whether that's true, I think you'd be safer with me than anywhere else. In fact, I think I should stay right here and sleep on your couch tonight."

He watched her as he spoke, watched the way her eyes darkened to a deeper shade of blue and how she nervously caught her lower lip between her teeth. Feeling her fear made his chest ache.

She slowly glanced toward his pistol, still lying on the coffee table, then looked back at him. "You really think I could end up dead, don't you."

"I won't let that happen." He gazed at her, the lush fullness of her mouth making him wish she wasn't involved with her Brian.

"Promise?"

"Promise," he said. Then, knowing it was a dangerous thing to do, he drew her into his arms and held her close.

Her body was so warm and enticing that he could feel his blood running hot and his heart thudding against his ribs. She smelled better than he could remember a woman ever smelling, and the way her hair was softly tickling his cheek was erotic as hell.

He reminded himself again about Brian. If she was serious about the guy, she'd have no interest in another man. Which meant that any other man who got interested in her would be riding for a fall. So why on earth was he holding her like this?

He tried telling himself it was only because she

was frightened, but he'd never been much good at self-deception.

"You're sure you wouldn't mind staying the night?" she murmured at last.

Closing his eyes, he tried to ignore the rush of arousal sweeping through him. And tried not to wish she was asking him about staying in an entirely different context.

BETH WOKE TO THE combination of Bogey purring like a motor and his cold little nose pushing against hers.

She sleepily opened her eyes, recollections of the day before streaming into her consciousness. That had her wide awake in seconds, but at least the so-afraid-it-hurt feeling had been banished by a good night's sleep.

Momentarily, she wondered if she'd have gotten any sleep if Cole hadn't stayed with her. Then, reaching over, she pressed the button to open the skylight's louvered blind.

Seconds later, sunshine began spilling into the bedroom. And as was so often true, things seemed a lot better in the bright light of day. Not, she thought sardonically, that they could possibly seem much worse.

From the foot of the bed, Bacall wailed a demand for breakfast.

"You know, you could use a little of Bogey's subtlety," she said, swinging her feet to the floor and cautiously putting a bit of weight on her ankle. Surprisingly, it seemed fine.

When Bacall gave another plaintive "meeeeow,"

Beth tugged on her robe and started across the room, both cats at her heels.

Quietly, she opened the bedroom door and looked over to where Cole was still sprawled asleep on the couch—half-naked, with the top of the sheet bunched down around his waist and one bare arm hanging over the side of the couch.

Without consciously thinking about it, she moved closer, her eyes lingering on him.

His hair was tousled, and the little laugh lines beside his eyes were less pronounced in sleep. The rugged angles of his face, darkened by an overnight growth of beard, didn't look quite as chiseled as they had yesterday.

She let herself continue to gaze at him—even though the warmth she felt flowing through her said it wasn't the wisest of ideas.

He had broader shoulders than she'd realized, his arms and chest were firmly muscled, and there was just a nice dusting of brown hair on his chest. She found that attractive. She'd never understood why some women liked male chests that were as hairy as apes'.

"Meeeeow," Bacall said loudly.

Cole opened his eyes and gazed over at Beth.

Her pulse skipped about sixteen beats. Between that growth of beard and his lazy, not-quite-fully-awake expression, he looked sexy as all get-out.

"Sorry," she said. "I was going to let you sleep until I'd had my shower."

"Good idea," he mumbled, rolling onto his side and tugging the sheet up so far that his entire head was covered.

Turning away, she headed into the kitchen and fed

the cats. Then she hit the shower. By the time she'd dried her hair, she could smell coffee brewing, and when she emerged from the bathroom, Cole was sitting on one of the stools at the kitchen counter.

His hands were wrapped around a mug and one of the sheets was wrapped around him. The effect of that was too sexy to be legal.

"Coffee?" he said.

She smiled, trying not to wonder if he had anything at all on under that sheet. "You're a handy man to have around."

"I do my best." He reached for the coffeepot and poured some for her. "I'll shower and shave at my apartment," he added, handing her the mug. "We'll have to go by there, anyway, so I can put on a fresh suit before we head for Abbot's."

"Right," she said, wishing he hadn't reminded her about the morning's plans.

Maybe she *had* agreed to go and talk to Abbot, but her desire to be part of this investigation hadn't been magically reborn overnight.

She was just about to have another shot at convincing him he should see Abbot alone when someone knocked on the door.

He glanced toward the office, then at her. "You expecting anyone?"

She shook her head.

Gathering the sheet more securely around himself, he slid off the stool. "Let's go see who it is."

"After yesterday, it might be my mother," she said, eyeing the sheet.

Without another word, he headed into the living room and pulled his suit pants on beneath the sheet.

Then he tossed it onto the couch, reaching for his shirt as the someone knocked again.

Nervously, Beth led the way through her office and checked the peephole. "It's just my neighbor from across the hall."

When she opened the door, Marlon Birch gave her the slow smile he figured was a turn-on. Then he caught sight of Cole in the apartment doorway and the smile vanished. "Oh, this isn't your *other* friend. What's-his-name."

"No, it's not," Beth said, refusing to give him the satisfaction of seeing how the remark annoyed her.

"Well, sorry, didn't know you had company. But I'm out of coffee."

"Sure, no problem." She introduced the two men and started for the kitchen while they stood sizing each other up—Cole in bare feet and still buttoning his shirt, Marlon wearing only a pair of low-slung denim cutoffs.

Grabbing the can of coffee from the counter, she checked that she had an unopened one in the cupboard, then hurried back to her office.

"I really will go shopping one of these days," Marlon said, taking the can.

"I think I've heard that before."

He grinned, shot Cole a final, appraising look, and turned toward his own apartment.

"What does he do when he's dressed?" Cole said as she closed the door.

"He plays guitar in a band. And he usually sleeps days and works nights, so I don't see a lot of him."

"But he's an all-right guy?"

"Well…actually, he's pretty obnoxious. He figures he's God's gift to women."

"Oh? Has he ever asked you out or anything?"

"More like 'anything.' And he was pretty insistent about it—and pretty incensed when I made it clear I wasn't interested. I don't think his ego takes kindly to being turned down."

"You seem on friendly enough terms now."

She shrugged. "He stayed angry for a while, but he runs out of things a lot. And I'd rather be friends with my neighbors. As long as he doesn't try to get too friendly again."

THE ENTIRE WAY UP Duplex Avenue, Cole kept glancing in the rearview mirror.

The fact that he obviously thought someone might be following them had Beth's anxiety level sky-high. Then he caught her watching him and smiled. It was nothing more than a friendly smile, but it made her feel less nervous. It also made her suddenly warm— a fact she did her best to ignore.

"We should get to Abbot's in good time," he said, glancing at his watch.

"I had my doubts when you took so long in the shower," she told him.

That made him smile again. This time, she looked away. His smiles not only made her warm, they also did something funny to her insides. The man had an animal magnetism that she seemed to be growing less and less able to ignore.

Or maybe she was completely misreading her re-actions. After all, she might not be certain that Brian was her Mr. Forever, but she was pretty sure she loved him. So maybe the pull she felt toward Cole was simply a function of the fact that he made her feel protected.

After all, last night, when she'd been so upset and frightened, his holding her had made all the difference in the world. Snuggled against him, she'd felt as if nothing could harm her.

But that was hardly the same as being attracted to him, and confusing the two would be a dumb, dumb thing to do. Which meant the only smart thing was to keep in mind that theirs was a business relationship—and to be careful she didn't let it become anything more.

Just as she finished sorting that issue out in her head, he glanced at her and smiled once more. Not merely with his mouth, but with his eyes, and with those little laugh lines, and with the angle of his jaw.

Her heart skipped a beat. At the moment, he was making her feel anything but safe.

"This is the street," he said, flicking on his turn signal.

Roselawn was one of the more modest streets in the tony district of North Toronto. Still, the mostly brick houses were attractive and well kept. As Cole swung the Mustang into the driveway of one of them, she took a deep breath.

He cut the ignition and glanced at her. "Ready?"

"I guess. But what about last night? Do we tell him about the shooter?"

"No. We're on a fact-finding mission, so it's better not to say anything that might get us off track. Especially not when he's got a plane to catch." Reaching over, Cole gave her hand a quick squeeze. "You'll do fine."

She felt a tiny flutter near her heart. It made her wonder why she never felt anything like that at Brian's touch—and made her afraid that, deep down, she knew exactly why.

Chapter Seven

Practically the first thing Frank Abbot said to Beth was that he'd questioned her while he was actively investigating Larisa's murder. She didn't recall him, but that was hardly surprising. He'd have been about forty then, and now he was in his early sixties.

A large man, with only a gray fringe of hair, he had piercing blue eyes that both belied his age and made her feel more than a little intimidated. Still, she'd managed to get through her story.

"I guess that's everything," she concluded.

Except, of course, that the murderer had been wearing her father's face. But she had no intention of telling Abbot that. As planned, she'd simply said she hadn't recalled the killer's face.

When she glanced at Cole, his nod of approval made her feel slightly less nervous.

"What do you think?" he asked Frank. "Does what she's recalled mesh with the facts?"

"Perfectly."

The word made her stomach lurch. If everything else she'd remembered was right... But no, her father just *couldn't* have been the killer. Whatever else was right, that part had to be wrong.

"The victim and the murderer were standing precisely where she remembers seeing them," Frank explained. "Plus, the killer *was* wearing sneakers and a white terry-cloth robe."

"You knew that?" Beth whispered.

"Uh-huh. We found bloodstained fiber evidence from the robe. But only in the area where the stabbing actually took place—even though, afterward, the killer went down the hall to shower. So the logical explanation was that he'd removed the robe before walking away from the body. And your recollection confirms that."

"You're saying *he*," Cole said. "Is there any chance the killer was a woman?"

Beth glanced at him, curious about why he'd asked that.

"It's possible," Frank told him. "As a matter of fact, one of the people we questioned was a woman."

"Really?" Cole's expression was suddenly very strange. He looked as if he half wanted Frank to tell him all about the female suspect and half didn't want to hear another word. So what was the story?

"Mrs. Niebuhr was short and slight," Frank was saying. "About five foot two?" he asked Beth.

She shook her head. "I remember her as shorter than my mother, but I was only eight. All adults seemed tall to me."

"Well, she was...I guess *petite*'s the word," Frank said, focusing on Cole again. "So the killer certainly could have been a woman. The stab wounds didn't indicate a particularly strong individual. But we ruled out our female suspect. And now, of course, it's a man Beth remembers seeing.

"What we did know, from the angles of the wounds, was that the killer was right-handed and somewhere between about five foot seven and five-eleven. As far as physical description goes, that's all we had.

"At any rate, getting back to the bathrobe, we were never sure exactly what he'd done with it, but Beth's remembering the garbage bag gives me that piece of the puzzle.

"As for knowing he was wearing sneakers, he tracked blood with them. Men's size nine. I suppose he eventually put them in the bag, too, because there was no evidence he was wearing them when he left the house."

"Do you know what he *was* wearing?" Cole asked.

"We assumed the clothes he'd arrived in. As for shoes, I don't know for sure, but I always had a feeling he brought extra ones with him."

"So he just walked out of the house carrying a garbage bag? And on a street like Tranby nobody noticed?"

Frank shook his head. "I don't think he was carrying the bag when he left. I mean, not that anybody would have seen. A sports bag of Dr. Niebuhr's was missing, and we figure he used it to take the evidence away in."

"So, when you add everything up... Frank, you didn't really believe the unknown-intruder theory at all, did you? I mean, when you figure a killer's done something as premeditated as bringing along an extra pair of shoes and a bathrobe, he—"

"No, *that* he didn't bring with him. Dr. Niebuhr

owned a white terry-cloth robe that was also missing after the murder.''

"Oh, Lord," Beth murmured, feeling decidedly queasy. "He killed Larisa wearing Mark's robe? That's— I can't even think of a word for what that is."

"*Macabre* always seemed an appropriate one to me," Frank offered.

Cole shot her a sympathetic glance. "Are you okay with this?"

She hesitated. He was offering her the out he'd promised. But she'd hung in this far, and surely things couldn't get any worse. "I'm fine," she said.

Cole's gaze lingered on her for another second, then he looked at Frank once more. "What about the drains? Any useful evidence from his shower?"

"Uh-uh. We were hoping for hair, of course, but the guy was either really careful or really lucky."

"Or bald."

Frank barked a laugh. "Yeah, we thought of that, too. At any rate, the only hair we found had come from the Niebuhrs.

"But look," he said to Beth. "Before we get into any more of this, let me ask you about something else. I got on the Internet last night and did some research on recovered memories. And a lot of experts figure that facts people have picked up over the years get all mixed up with what they ultimately recall.

"So, with your mother knowing details the general public didn't, and your uncle knowing even more of them, how much had you been told before that memory finally surfaced?"

She slowly shook her head. "I really didn't know anything more than I'd read in those newspaper articles. After I decided I wanted to make myself remember, I did try talking to my mother. But she just got upset. And my uncle... Well, he'd never talked to me about the murder and I'd never asked him to."

"You mean, over the years, you all...acted like it had never happened?"

"No. We just never really talked about it. But on the anniversary of Larisa's death, we always take flowers to her grave, and—"

"The anniversary of her death. July 27. That's tomorrow."

Beth nodded, wondering if she'd find tomorrow's visit to the cemetery even more difficult than usual.

"Okay, then," Frank continued, "can you remember anything about what the killer looked like?"

"No," she said, not meeting either Frank's gaze or Cole's.

"Well, do you have any sense of whether you'd seen him before that day?"

"No."

"Might she have?" Cole said.

Frank shrugged. "Maybe. You were right about my never really believing the unknown-intruder theory. That was just a public relations ploy.

"The case was dragging on and we hadn't laid any charges. Hell, we didn't even have the murder weapon. The killer took that with him, too. So PR put out the unknown-intruder story because the public was demanding to know why we weren't getting anywhere.

"But to answer your question, if the killer did know Mrs. Niebuhr, it's possible Beth had seen him before. She spent a fair amount of time at the Niebuhrs' house."

Beth held her breath, waiting to see where Frank would go from there. When he said nothing more, she exhaled slowly, telling herself if he'd suspected her father, that had been the perfect time to say so.

Deep down, though, she knew his silence might not mean a thing.

Finally, he glanced at Cole and said, "Why don't I run through some of the facts that might help you?"

"Great."

"Well, you probably read in one of those articles that a screen had been removed from an open kitchen window. But the dust on the ledge wasn't disturbed, which meant the killer was just trying to mislead us and actually came in through a door."

"But all the doors were locked," Beth said.

Cole looked at her.

"I've always remembered everything that happened *before* the murder," she reminded him. "And Larisa and I checked all the doors before we went up to the attic."

Frank nodded. "According to Niebuhr, his wife was pretty obsessive about keeping the doors locked. And there was no sign of forced entry. So, assuming they all were locked, the killer had a key."

"And who had keys?" Cole asked.

"That was our problem. Basically, only the Niebuhrs. They'd given a front door key to Angela Gregory, but that was it.

"Your mother had misplaced hers," he added to Beth. "It didn't turn up until weeks after the murder, which is why she couldn't just unlock the front door when she got there and nobody answered."

"But she found the back door unlocked because

the killer left through it,'' Beth said, thinking she must have those articles memorized word for word.

"Right,'' Frank agreed. "At any rate, the question of who could have gotten his hands on a key was an important one. So after we ruled out the husband as a suspect, we—''

"What? My uncle was one of your suspects?''

Frank quickly shook his head. "Not really. We were able to eliminate him right away. He was in his office all morning. His secretary confirmed that.

"So then we checked out the locksmith who'd installed the locks. The Niebuhrs had new ones installed when they bought the house. At any rate, the locksmith came up clean, so we started questioning other people who might have gotten access to a key. By the time we were done, we'd questioned several people who'd known the victim—and who might have had a motive to murder her. But we never came up with solid evidence pointing to anyone we suspected.''

"And who were your suspects?'' Cole asked.

Frank looked at Beth once more. This time, his gaze made her hands grow clammy and started cold sweat trickling down between her breasts.

He was going to say that her father had been one of them. And would that mean her recollection hadn't confused his face with the killer's?

"Beth?'' Cole said. "Are you sure you're okay with this? Do you want to wait outside?''

The trickle of sweat had become a stream. Cole knew what Frank was about to tell them as well as she did.

"No, I'm all right,'' she said, forcing the words out. "Whoever the suspects were, I want to know.''

"Well," Frank said slowly, "it's not so much *who* the suspects were that might bother you."

"What, then?"

He glanced at Cole.

"If she didn't want to hear, she'd leave," he said.

She held her breath, waiting for Frank to go on. She didn't want to hear, yet she had to.

LOOKING RELUCTANT, ABBOT finally clasped his hands on his desk and leaned forward.

Cole glanced at Beth, wondering if he should have tried to press her into leaving. He didn't know what was coming, but Abbot seemed damned uneasy about the prospect of telling them.

"Well, Beth," he said, "the thing is that your aunt had numerous…involvements. Quite frequently, she'd have a male visitor while Dr. Niebuhr was at his office."

"What?" she whispered. "You mean she was having affairs?"

Abbot cleared his throat. "I guess that depends on how you define 'affair.' According to the neighbors, Mrs. Niebuhr would sometimes have more than one man visiting her within brief spans of time. In any event, we were able to identify all but one of the men she'd been seeing before her death, and these men were our prime suspects in the case."

Beth simply stared across Abbot's desk as if she couldn't believe what the man had said. When she finally looked at Cole, his heart went out to her. Given the way she talked about Larisa, she'd obviously idolized her. And learning her idol hadn't been Snow White had clearly shaken her.

"Did Mark know?" she finally asked. "About the men?"

"Only after we told him," Abbot said. "Once we'd established that your aunt *had* been intimate with them, we had to talk to Dr. Niebuhr and see if there was anything useful he could tell us.

"I'd assumed he must have had at least some idea of what she'd been up to, but he was completely shocked. In fact, she'd actually told him about two of the men coming to the house, and he thought their visits were perfectly innocent."

"You've got to be kidding," Cole said.

Abbot shrugged. "I guess Mrs. Niebuhr was pretty convincing. She claimed she was having problems with her back, which explained one of the guys. He was a massage therapist. The other one she told Niebuhr about was a Spanish teacher—supposedly giving her private lessons."

"And they were two out of how many?" Cole said.

"During the year before her death, there were at least three others. Two, we were able to identify and question. And, as I said, there was one we couldn't ID. One of the neighbors had seen him a couple of times. Three, to be precise. But her description was too generic to be much help. You know the kind—average height and weight, brown hair, somewhere in his thirties."

Cole nodded. The description might be generic, but it would have fit Glen Gregory.

"The neighbor had never gotten a good enough look at the guy to help a police artist," Abbot continued. "And the only unusual thing she noticed about him—which really wasn't too unusual in the seventies—was that he had a ponytail. And that all three times she saw him he was wearing a hat of some sort.

"Of course, the ponytail might not have been for real. And when you factor in the hats, it ups the odds on that. At any rate, we were never able to track him down. But look, I've made up a couple of lists for you."

He passed several sheets of paper across his desk. "The first one's pretty exhaustive—most of the people our investigative team spent any time talking to. A lot of the addresses will be out of date, but it'll give you a start. And this is a list of our suspects." Abbot picked up another sheet of paper and handed it over.

It was a computer printout headed Prime Suspects. Cole held it halfway over to Beth, so she could see it as well, and scanned the list of names:

Juan Perez
Anthony Bridges
Charles Mantay
William Colburn
Susan Colburn
Unidentified White Male

Cole's gaze flickered back up from Unidentified White Male to the name Susan Colburn.

He'd assumed the female suspect had been Angela Gregory, and it surprised him that he'd been wrong. Or had Susan Colburn not really been the only female suspect?

Maybe Abbot had decided against telling Beth they'd suspected her mother. For that matter, maybe he'd decided not to mention they'd suspected her father.

Cole wanted to ask, but not in front of her. He'd phone Abbot later, before he and his wife left for the airport.

"Juan Perez, as you've probably guessed from his name," Abbot said, "was the Spanish teacher. And Mrs. Niebuhr wasn't the first of his students he'd done more than give lessons to.

"Bridges was the massage therapist. Charles Mantay was a writer who worked in a bookstore—but only evenings, so he had free time during the day.

"William Colburn was a salesman for a food company. Mrs. Niebuhr met him in a grocery store. And Susan Colburn was his wife."

"And she made your list because…?" Cole asked.

"Because her husband had a habit of meeting women in grocery stores, and Susan had found out about his previous affair. She'd told him the next one would be his last—that if he ever played around on her again, she'd kill both him and the woman."

"But you knew the killer was wearing men's sneakers," Beth said.

"That didn't mean it had to be a man. Now that you've remembered it was, it puts a different perspective on things. At the time, though… Well, Susan Colburn wasn't exactly a stable woman, and her murdering someone wasn't beyond the realm of the believable."

"But you never charged her?" Cole said. "Or anyone else on the list?"

Abbot shook his head. "We ended up ruling out everyone except the mystery man, as we used to call him. As far as Susan was concerned, she was shopping with a friend on the morning of the murder.

"Of course, there was the possibility she'd hired somebody to do the hit. Hell, any of them could have done that, and we followed up hard on that. We put out the word to every snitch in town, but it didn't get us anything except false leads.

"At any rate, there was a weak link in the theory that Susan might have hired a hit man. We were convinced the killer used a key to get into the Niebuhrs' house. And where would she have gotten one to give him?"

"Her husband didn't have one?" Cole asked.

"He swore he didn't, and it was probably true. We asked each of the suspects if Mrs. Niebuhr had ever given them a key, and they all told us she hadn't. Not that one of them couldn't have taken a key and had it copied, but we just couldn't see Susan getting hold of one.

"As for the male suspects, all four of the ones we identified denied still being involved with Mrs. Niebuhr at the time of the murder. They all said they hadn't seen her in weeks."

"Did you believe them?"

Abbot shrugged. "The same neighbor who told us about our mystery man, an Esther Voise, said she hadn't seen any of the others around recently. That hardly proved they hadn't been there, but two of them had iron-clad alibis for the time of the murder. Perez was teaching classes, and Bridges was booked with clients.

"William Colburn, who claimed that he and Larisa had broken things off as soon as Susan found out about them, was working that morning—making his regular calls.''

"Driving around the city, you mean," Cole said.

"Yeah, so he could have stopped by the Niebuhrs' house. But it would have been impossible for him to have been there long enough to have murdered Mrs. Niebuhr and gotten cleaned up. His customers all remembered him being in their stores, and his schedule was too tight for him to have been our man.

"Which left Charles Mantay and the mystery man. Mantay's story was that he was at home, writing.''

"He have anyone to corroborate that?''

"No, but we couldn't come up with a motive, and he claimed that he and Mrs. Niebuhr had parted amicably. So with nothing really pointing to him, and no apparent motive, we'd reached a dead end there, too.

"That meant we were down to our mystery man. Since we'd eliminated everyone else, we figured he must have done it. That he'd somehow gotten a key and just walked right in. Unless, of course, Mrs. Niebuhr hadn't checked the doors as well as she thought, and the murderer really was an unknown intruder.''

"Who brought along an extra pair of shoes?" Cole said.

Abbot merely shrugged again, but he'd already told them that he'd never really believed the unknown-intruder theory.

WHEN COLE AND BETH left Frank Abbot's, both Frank and his wife walked them down the driveway, explaining that they were on their way out to have brunch before they headed for the airport.

So much, Cole thought, for his idea of phoning

Abbot to ask if either of Beth's parents had been suspects. It probably didn't matter, though. Not when Abbot had confirmed that Beth's recollection of the murder was in line with the facts.

That had to make it almost a certainty her father had been the killer. If every other detail she'd remembered was accurate, why on earth would she have confused her father's face with the murderer's? But the sixty-million-dollar question, in Cole's mind, was how hard would she take it if they found proof of her father's guilt? Hell, he didn't want to even think about that.

After thanking Abbot again for his help, and telling the couple to enjoy their trip, he backed out of the driveway and started down the street. Then, while Beth turned to wave a final goodbye, his imagination began playing with the scenario of Glen Gregory as the mystery man.

A woman with the sexual appetite Larisa had apparently had wouldn't likely have kept her hands off Gregory simply because he was her brother-in-law. Especially not when, according to Niebuhr, the Gregorys' marriage had been on the rocks.

So, if Gregory had been having an affair with Larisa, and for some reason had decided he wanted her dead...

He'd even had ready access to a key. Angela Gregory's key to the Niebuhr's front door probably hadn't been misplaced at all. Far more likely, Glen Gregory had taken it.

"Cole?" Beth said.

He looked over at her.

"You're thinking the mystery man could have been my father, aren't you."

"Well...I've got to admit the thought crossed my mind." The moment the words were out, he was glad he hadn't said he was almost positive, because even his low-key reply was enough to start tears trickling down her face.

"Oh, Cole," she whispered. "It crossed my mind, too." She wiped the tears away, but they were immediately replaced by more.

He turned onto the next side street and pulled up to the curb. "Would you like to talk about it?"

"I don't know," she said, digging some tissues out of her purse.

She looked so miserable that he wanted to take her in his arms, the way he had last night. But he resisted. Holding her the first time had been a mistake.

After she'd finally gone to bed, he'd lain awake for hours, wishing the soft warmth of her body was still pressed against him, and that her fresh-meadow scent was still in the air. And while he'd been tossing and turning on the couch, thoughts of Brian Robertson had begun nagging at him.

It had been a long, long time since he'd felt the kind of attraction he was feeling toward Beth. And he sure as hell didn't want to let the feeling get any stronger if she was really serious about some other guy. He'd like to just come right out and ask where things stood between her and this Brian, but it was hardly a good time to ask about her love life.

Giving her eyes another wipe, she said, "I just... Frank Abbot is certain the mystery man was the murderer, isn't he?"

"I don't think he has much doubt."

She slowly shook her head. "You know, part of me still can't believe there's even a chance my father killed Larisa. Most of me can't. But if everything else I remembered is right..."

Her words, of course, were echoing what he'd been thinking, but he kept his mouth shut. It would be better to let her arrive at her own conclusions.

"Our shooter," she said at last. "How tall was he?"

"Average height."

"I knew you'd say that," she murmured. "But I was still hoping you'd tell me he was five foot one, or six foot nine. And I suppose he was average weight, too?"

Cole simply nodded.

"And he probably had brown hair."

"Don't most gorillas?" When he smiled, she smiled back. But her smile looked even more forced than his felt. And that was hardly surprising.

Last night, Glen Gregory had pulled away from the restaurant before they'd even headed for the parking lot. Which meant he'd have had plenty of time to reach Wilson Place before they did. Of course, the idea of his trying to kill his own daughter... But if he was doing it to save his skin... And since they weren't really close...

"The shooter couldn't have been my father," Beth said. "He didn't know I'd remembered a thing until I told him. And you and I agreed that he certainly wouldn't have been driving around with coveralls and a gorilla mask in his car."

"Well, I sure didn't think it was likely," Cole said slowly. "But I wouldn't go as far as to say it was impossible."

Beth's eyes grew dark with fresh tears. "How can we even be speculating along these lines? How can

I be thinking it's even possible that my father had an affair with my mother's sister? And then murdered her? And that he tried to murder me before I could remember too much?

"Cole, I just can't deal with any of those assumptions. He wouldn't have had an affair with Larisa and he couldn't have killed her. There has to be some other explanation."

"Well...maybe there is."

"You really think so?"

She looked as if she was absolutely desperate to believe he did, so he said, "There could be. Abbot said that writer, Charles Mantay, had no one who could corroborate that he was home at the time of the murder."

"But he had no motive."

"None that the police could establish. He's certainly worth talking to, though. And there was the possibility of a hit man. We'll keep that in mind, too. But the important thing, right now, is that Abbot figured the killer did know Larisa. Which means he's got to know who you are. So, as I said last night, if he somehow did find out you were trying to remember..."

Beth's tense expression said he didn't have to elaborate further. There was no longer much—if any—doubt that their gorilla man had been specifically after her.

"Oh, Cole," she said. "I just don't know if I can take any more of this." With that, she began crying again. But it wasn't the "tears trickling down her cheeks" variety. It was the heartfelt sobbing of a woman who felt emotionally stretched to the limit.

This time Cole didn't resist. He shifted over to the

edge of his seat and wrapped his arms around her. And when she buried her face against his chest, he rested his chin on the top of her head and began stroking her silky hair.

"It's going to be okay," he said, once she'd finally cried herself out. "We'll make it be okay."

"How?" she whispered, drawing back and looking at him. "What are we going to do?"

"Well, first, we're going to stop by my apartment again and I'll pick up some clothes. The way things stand, it only makes sense for me to stay at your place until we get this sorted out.

"And I've got a couple of things to clean up for other clients when I get the chance, so I want to hit my office and pick up my laptop and a few files. After that, we'll go back to your place and get to work. And we'll just keep at it until we figure out who killed Larisa."

"And if we can't?"

"We will."

Beth sat gazing at him, her eyes still shimmering with tears. "But if we can't," she murmured at last, "he's going to kill me, isn't he."

"I promised I wouldn't let anything awful happen to you, remember?"

She slowly shook her head. "I hope you're a man of your word, Cole. I hope it with all my heart."

Chapter Eight

When Beth and Cole finally got back to her apartment—after collecting everything he figured he'd need and then stopping for lunch—there was a message to phone her mother. But all she got when she returned the call was her mother's machine.

After leaving her own message, saying she'd call again later, she put down fresh water for the cats while Cole phoned in for his voice mail. Then she stood surveying the things he'd brought with him— some clothes, a shaving kit, his laptop, a printer and a briefcase.

Mere days ago, if someone had told her that a man she'd barely met would be moving in with her, she'd have said they were crazy.

But here she was, and there he was. And she was only too glad to have him with her.

"I've got to return a couple of calls," he said from across the room.

And after that, she knew, he'd be phoning Esther Voise—the neighbor who'd told the police about the mystery man.

Cole had decided she'd be the ideal person to talk

to first. So while he'd been collecting his things at his place, Beth had checked the phone book.

According to it, E. Voise still lived in the same house on Tranby Street, almost directly across from the house that had been Mark and Larisa's.

"Don't forget about the picture," Cole said.

She nodded, resisting the temptation to say she hadn't been able to forget about it for more than three seconds straight since he'd told her he wanted it.

Wandering into her bedroom, she opened the closet door and dug out one of the old photograph albums she'd gotten from her mother, unable to keep from wishing that she'd never looked at any of them in the first place. Maybe, if she hadn't seen all those snapshots of Larisa...

Telling herself she couldn't undo what was already done, she took the album into the living room and sat, reluctantly flipping through it, looking for a good picture of her father. Cole, she could hear, had gotten hold of Esther Voise and was asking if he could drop by and talk to her.

"Four-thirty or five?" he said. "Sure, that would be great. Oh, and I'll have an associate with me."

An associate. She'd been promoted from unpaid assistant to associate. But at this point, she'd far rather be nothing. Nada. Completely out of the investigation. And that included not being in charge of finding a suitable picture.

Turning over another couple of pages, she reached a snapshot of her father standing alone. Deciding it would do, she slid it out from beneath the plastic covering and put it on the coffee table. Then she sat staring at the other picture on that page, the one of her with him, and let her thoughts drift back in time.

The picture had been taken on Centre Island, in front of an enormous weeping willow. In it, she was holding her father's hand and smiling for the camera. He wasn't smiling—likely because the person on the other side of the camera had been her mother—but it was still a nice picture of him.

"How old were you there?" Cole asked, sinking down beside her on the couch. "About ten?"

"Good guess. It was my tenth birthday."

"Yeah? I can still remember my tenth birthday. My parents took me and a bunch of friends horseback riding. I think they figured it would be easier on the house than a regular party. But we all ended up hardly able to walk—which my sisters thought was hilarious."

She managed a smile. "How many sisters?"

"Two."

"Older than you?"

"No, both younger."

"I always used to wish I had sisters," she said, looking back at the snapshot. "I didn't like being an only child—especially not after my parents called it quits. That was only a month or so after this picture was taken."

"I guess that's a bad age to have your parents break up," he said gently.

"I guess any age is. What about you and your wife? Any children?" As she asked, she remembered she'd intended to keep her relationship with Cole strictly a business one. But it seemed the better she got to know him, the more she wanted to know about him. And it was nice to be talking about something normal for a change, instead of about nightmares and murders and a man in a gorilla mask shooting at her.

"No, no children," Cole was saying. "Joanne, my ex-wife, didn't want any."

"Oh? The way you said that... You mean, she didn't but you did?"

"Yeah, I like kids."

"Me, too."

"Yeah?"

When he smiled, she found herself trying to picture what he'd looked like as a little boy—and what any children he might some day have would look like.

Cute, she decided. They'd be cute, smart little kids with deep hazel eyes and adorable smiles.

"Joanne wanted a career instead of kids," he continued. "I know it's something we should have talked about before we got married, but it didn't even occur to me she might not want to be a mother."

"And that was why you broke up?"

"Not entirely," he said slowly. "Maybe, if that had been the only problem, we'd have worked out some sort of compromise.

"But I was still a cop back then, and shift work can be pretty hard on a marriage. Plus, Joanne was really ambitious—always working late, then taking classes a couple of nights a week. So between her schedule and mine, we'd often go for days at a stretch barely seeing each other, and... Well, somewhere along the way, while we weren't spending much time together, we drifted completely apart."

"I'm sorry. Enough of my friends have been through a divorce that I know how tough it is."

He shrugged. "I'm over it now. And she's remarried, so she obviously is, too."

Beth hesitated, telling herself to stop right there.

But she couldn't keep from going on. "She's remarried and you haven't. Does that mean you've sworn off marriage?"

She'd tried to make the words sound nonchalant, but when Cole simply gazed at her she knew he'd seen right through her. The question had been painfully transparent. So why in the world had she asked it?

Because you're interested in him, an imaginary voice whispered. *You aren't drawn to him merely because he makes you feel protected. There's far more to it than that, and you might as well admit it. Trying to deny what you're feeling isn't going to make it go away.*

"No," he said at last. "I haven't sworn off marriage. I expect that, some day, I'll fall for someone else. I'll just have to make sure it's a someone who wants to spend a little more time having fun than Joanne did. And a someone who doesn't have a Brian in her life."

Cole was gazing at her again, and this time she grew positively hot. He was the one asking a question now. Maybe not aloud, but she could see it in his eyes. And she didn't know how she should answer it.

He shrugged, just a little too casually, and said, "When Brian phoned, and you were screening the call, I couldn't help overhear him call you 'love.' So I assumed things were pretty serious between the two of you."

Now the question was right out in the open, and hearing him say it had started heat curling low in her belly. He wouldn't have asked it if he wasn't interested in her—in exactly the same way she was interested in him.

She searched for the right words, still not entirely sure what she wanted to say. She'd thought she was in love with Brian. But right this moment she was wondering if she'd merely been trying to convince herself of that.

He was a nice man. They had a lot in common and she enjoyed being with him. But if she was really *in love* with him, how could Cole be practically melting her with his eyes?

"I guess Brian and I are at that stage where we're not quite sure how serious things are," she said at last.

"Oh? You mean that stage where things could go either way?"

"Aah…yes, I guess you could put it like that." She felt a stab of guilt as she spoke—almost as if she were betraying Brian. Then Cole caught her gaze once more, and it made her pulse begin to race.

She'd never before met anyone who could send hot rushes through her by merely looking at her. And now that she had, she was going to have to do some good, hard thinking about how much she really did care for Brian.

Maybe the pull she felt toward Cole meant that she'd been dragging her feet with Brian because, deep down, she'd known he wasn't the right one for her. But until she'd had a chance to think things through, she'd be a whole lot wiser to stick to more neutral ground with Cole.

Closing the album, she reached for the photograph she'd put on the coffee table, forcing her thoughts back to where they'd been before they'd gotten so far off track.

"This would probably be a good one," she said.

"It looks fine."

"But I hate this, you know. I feel as if I'm persecuting him," she added, handing the snapshot to Cole.

"I know."

"Then why can't we start with someone else?"

"Beth...you heard what Abbot said. Two of their suspects had iron-clad alibis, the timing would have been impossible for William Colburn, and they couldn't see how his wife could conceivably have been the one.

"That means the only sensible places to start are either with Charles Mantay, the one without a solid alibi, or Mrs. Voise, who might be able to help us ID the mystery man."

"Then why don't we start with Mantay?" She caught Cole's gaze once more and held it, wondering if he'd tell her the truth—tell her that he'd decided to start by trying to ID the mystery man because he was certain it was Glen Gregory.

Cole might still be *saying* her father wasn't necessarily guilty, but she knew he figured that possibility was awfully remote.

"We'll get to Mantay," he said at last. "I already told you we'd talk to him. But we don't have a current address for him, and we've got one for Esther Voise. So starting with her is only logical."

Maybe it was. But what would happen when they showed her the photograph?

What if she said, *Yes, that's the other man who used to visit Larisa. I couldn't describe him very well to the police, but I'm certain that's him. Even though he doesn't have a ponytail in this picture, I recognize him.*

Beth tried to imagine how hearing words like those would make her feel. Just thinking about it almost made her ill.

"I can't do this," she said.

"Can't do what?" Cole asked quietly.

"I can't go and see Esther Voise with you. I can't be there when you show her the picture.

"And you know what else? I don't think it's fair that you're doing it. It's like asking someone to look at a police lineup that has only one man in it."

"Beth—"

"And what if she *does* say it's a picture of the mystery man? She'll be remembering something from over twenty years ago. Even at the time she could hardly describe him."

Cole nodded. "You're right. Even if she says yes, that's the man, she could be wrong. But she might say he's *not* the man."

"And if she did? How much weight would you give that?"

"More than if she said it was him. Because your analogy to a police lineup with only one man in it was a good one."

But if Esther Voise *did* say the man in the picture was the man she'd seen those times...

Beth thought about that for a minute, then slowly shook her head. She was already completely strung out, and there was only so much she could put herself through. "Cole, I really don't want to go with you."

He eyed her for a long moment, then said, "Look, I think I've said this before—that I'm sorry I keep saying things that scare you. And I really am. But, under the circumstances, I don't want to leave you alone. Or with anyone else, for that matter. Not unless you'd like to hire a bodyguard.''

She could feel her heart thudding against her chest. He did keep scaring her, but she knew he had good reason for not wanting to leave her on her own. And she didn't really want him to.

''It sounds as if I already have a bodyguard,'' she finally said.

He smiled at that—a smile that crinkled the little lines beside his eyes and started a fluttering feeling inside her.

It made her aware that she wanted more than merely not being left on her own. She wanted to be with him. And it was definitely not only because he made her feel safe.

Lord, she had to do some good, hard thinking—and not with him sitting here on the couch beside her. Because, this close to him, she was having trouble thinking at all.

ONCE BETH FINALLY AGREED to go to Esther Voise's with him, Cole did his darnedest to steer the conversation back to a personal level.

After all, having two sisters had taught him something about women. And he knew that when one of them said, ''We're at the stage where we're not quite sure how serious things are,'' the guy she was referring to was hardly the love of her life.

So to hell with his rule about not mixing business with pleasure. Rules were made to be broken. He was sure somebody very wise had originally said that.

The problem was, Beth wasn't exactly being cooperative. In fact, he was barely getting warmed up when she said, "You know, I promised I'd try my mother again, so I think I'll go into my office and do it now. After that, I've got some work I really have to get to, and you..."

She paused, gesturing in the direction of his briefcase. "You have those things you want to clean up for other clients. Why don't you use the dining room table for work space?"

Since it was only too obvious that she meant "right now," he said, "Well...yeah, good idea. But before I do anything else, I think I'll make some notes about what Abbot told us."

With a quick nod, Beth disappeared around the glass brick wall that separated her office from the rest of the apartment.

Telling himself she hadn't actually been trying to get away from him, that she just wanted to keep busy because she was nervous about the prospect of visiting Esther Voise, Cole opened his laptop and started working.

When Beth eventually reappeared, something told him she didn't want to discuss anything that wasn't business-related, so he said, "I've got some news. I went into a few databases and managed to track down Charles Mantay. He's dead—died almost ten years ago."

"But...what if it was him?"

"Beth, the important issue is that whoever was taking potshots at you *isn't* dead. And it's far more likely that he killed Larisa than that Mantay did.

"Look," he continued, not wanting to dwell on the subject of killings, "it's a little early to head for

Esther Voise's, but do you think this would be a good time to phone your uncle?''

"Phone him?" she said uneasily.

"Yeah, he asked me to check in once a day, remember?"

She glanced at her watch, then said, "If you wait a couple of minutes, he'll probably be free. It's almost ten to four, and he does the standard fifty-minute hour with his patients. But...you're not thinking of saying anything about the shooter, are you? It would only worry him."

"No, I figured he could live without knowing."

"And you won't tell him I've remembered anything more."

"We already decided I wouldn't."

A flicker of relief crossed her face. "Right, I just thought you might have forgotten."

"Me? No way. I've got a memory like an elephant's."

"Oh? Really? Then why do you need to make so many notes? I could hear you on that laptop, and you were going a mile a minute."

He smiled. As he'd noticed before, when she wasn't scared half to death, she had a neat sense of humor.

Closing his laptop, he dug Niebuhr's card out of his wallet. He'd only glanced at it before, but now, looking more closely, he saw the address was on Bloor, right around Avenue Road.

"Your uncle's office is in a pretty high-rent district," he said, picking up Beth's cordless and punching in the number.

She nodded. "When he first rented it, he and Larisa were living in the Tranby house, which meant he could walk to work. So I guess he figured he'd save enough on parking to pay the extra rent.''

As she finished speaking, a woman answered Niebuhr's phone. When Cole told her who he was, she put him through without any questions. Niebuhr had obviously told her to expect the call.

"Cole," he said, coming on the line. "I'm glad to hear from you. What's been happening?"

"Oh, Beth and I have been pretty busy." He glanced at her. She'd sat down on the couch and wasn't even bothering to pretend she wasn't listening.

"We spent most of the morning with Frank Abbot," he told Niebuhr. "The detective who was in charge of the investigation."

"Yes, I remember Abbot. Did he tell you anything useful?"

"Uh-huh. There were a few things we'll be following up on."

"Really. I'd have thought the facts about a murder case would be highly confidential. Even after all this time."

"Well, I'm sure there were a lot of things he didn't tell us, but he got us off to a good start."

Niebuhr cleared his throat. "Did he…tell you who the suspects were?"

"He told us who some of the people they'd questioned were. But that's something I could have learned pretty easily on my own, so he didn't have any reason not to tell me."

There was a pause at the other end of the line before Niebuhr said, "Did he tell you some of them were…acquainted with Larisa?"

"Uh-huh. He mentioned a couple were people

she'd been seeing on a professional basis—a teacher of some sort? And a therapist?'' Cole stopped there, hoping he'd sounded believably vague about the details.

As Abbot had said, even if the big brass learned he'd discussed the case with a private investigator, and didn't like it, there wouldn't be much they could do. Still, Cole didn't want to risk getting the man into trouble.

''And exactly what will you be following up on?'' Niebuhr asked.

''Well, for starters, we've got an appointment to see one of your ex-neighbors in half an hour or so. An Esther Voise.''

''Yes, I remember her, as well. She was a nurse—although I imagine she retired long ago. And you're going to see her because…?''

Cole's glance flickered to the coffee table, to where the snapshot of Glen Gregory was lying. ''Oh, I just want to talk to her. That's what investigative work is all about—asking questions, seeing if you get anything interesting by way of answers.''

''Yes. Of course. And how's Beth doing?''

''Fine. Would you like to speak to her?''

''No, I just wondered if she'd remembered anything more. If what Frank Abbot told you had prompted further recollections.''

''No, she hasn't remembered anything more so far.'' Cole glanced at Beth as he delivered the lie. She rewarded him with a small smile. ''But you think she will?'' he added to Niebuhr.

''It's difficult to say. As I'm sure I told you, when it comes to the workings of the human mind, there are no certainties.''

After they'd said their goodbyes and Cole clicked the phone off, Beth said, "Thanks. I just... If we told him I *had* remembered more, and that it was all accurate..."

"Oh, I realize how badly I don't *want* to think my father might have done it. But there's more to it than that. I've got a feeling there's something about what I've remembered that... I can't seem to put it into words, but..."

"Woman's intuition?"

She gave him another small smile. "Maybe. Whatever it is, I just don't want to make Mark even more certain my father's guilty. Not unless we learn something that... Well, as I said yesterday, I don't think it would take much to make him go to the police on his own."

Which might be a damn good thing, Cole thought.

Or would it? What would happen if Niebuhr did go to the police?

The good doctor would say that Beth had remembered seeing her father murder Larisa, and that he'd hired a private investigator because she had—which would tell them that *he* was certainly giving Beth's memory a lot of credence.

And he'd undoubtedly warn them that Beth might not cooperate, that when they questioned her she might deny the truth. So how would the police proceed?

First, they *would* question Beth. And they'd question Cole, as well. Then, once they had, they'd tell him to butt out of *their* case.

All they'd have at that point, though, would be hearsay. That would be enough to make them question Glen Gregory. But unless he confessed, which was highly unlikely, they'd be forced to start digging for corroborative evidence—a darned tough job after so much time had passed.

The most important issue, Cole decided, uneasily rubbing his jaw, was who would be watching out for Beth while all that was going on?

Of course, if anything happened to her, Gregory would be the prime suspect. But what if he figured he'd be better off taking his chances with that than risk having his daughter testify as an eyewitness against him?

Then another possibility began snaking around in Cole's brain. What if, implausible as it might be, Gregory *wasn't* the killer? While the police were focusing on him, what would the real murderer be doing?

There wasn't much question about that. He'd be doing his damnedest to kill Beth—in case she remembered the face she'd actually seen.

Chapter Nine

"Beth?" Cole said as he turned onto Bedford Road. "Do you know your father's license plate?"

The question came straight out of the blue, and for a second she had no idea why he'd asked it.

Then, as he glanced into his rearview mirror, she had a horrible suspicion she knew.

Her heart began to pound even before she turned to look back. When she did, her throat went dry. A couple of cars behind them, ghostlike in the sunshine, was a silver BMW with darkly tinted windows.

Her father? Cole obviously thought so.

"Do you know the plate number?" he asked again.

She had to swallow hard before any words would come out. "No. Half the time I can't remember my own."

"Well let's try to get a look as this one goes by." He flicked on his signal and wheeled sharply into a private driveway.

The cars that had been behind them zipped past, including the BMW.

"Dammit," he muttered when it did.

Beth stared anxiously after it. A length of heavy

canvas was hanging out of the trunk and covering the rear plate.

"Where's a cop when you need one?" Cole muttered. "A concealed plate's a violation."

"Do you think it was my father?" she asked, desperately wanting him to say it probably wasn't. "I mean, there has to be more than one silver BMW in Toronto."

He shot her a wry glance. "Come on, Beth, an M3 coupe? Silver with black windows? How many of those can there be? And this one's definitely been tailing us. I noticed him a mile or so back, and he was only a couple of cars behind us all along Bloor."

Closing her eyes, she tried to think. She didn't want her father to have killed Larisa and she didn't want him to be tailing her, but her wanting didn't necessarily make it so.

"Why would he be following us?" she finally made herself ask.

"To see what we're up to."

But her father wasn't the sort of man who'd be following her. At least, she'd never have believed he was. Just as she'd never have believed he could be a murderer.

While a break in the traffic was allowing Cole to back out onto Bedford, the thought that she might be wrong on all counts flitted around the edges of her mind.

She tried to drive it away by exhaling a long, slow, calming breath. But before she'd even completely exhaled, they turned onto Tranby and her anxiety level climbed skyward again.

In the heart of one of Toronto's earliest upper-class neighborhoods, Tranby Avenue was charming—lined on both sides by big Victorian houses that, over the decades, had been either beautifully maintained or tastefully updated.

But Larisa had been murdered in one of them, and this was the first time, in all the years since, that Beth had ventured onto the street.

The nearer they drew to *that* house, the more unsettled she felt. She could visualize it—one of the larger ones, sitting about halfway along the north side of the block.

But she didn't dare look in its direction. Instead, she sat studiously gazing at the houses on the south side, checking the numbers as they neared Esther Voise's.

Just before they reached it, Cole stopped and backed into a space that at first glance seemed too small for the Mustang.

Fortunately, it wasn't, because, aside from it, the street was parked solid.

"Okay," he said, cutting the ignition. "She might know the name Beth Gregory, so use a phony one. We don't need her asking you questions."

As Beth nodded, he reached into the back seat for his briefcase—the briefcase containing the picture of her father as a young man.

Her stomach in knots, she climbed out of the car. A few more knots developed as they walked along to the house and she spotted a woman peering through one of the front windows.

She gave them a wave, then disappeared. A minute later, the front door opened and she was saying, "I'm Miss Voise, of course. Do come in."

A little bird of a woman, somewhere in her seventies, she seemed delighted to have visitors. Beth only wished she was even slightly delighted to be doing the visiting.

Cole introduced himself and gave the woman a business card, while Beth identified herself as Wendy Kinahan. Wendy was too good a friend to mind her name being used.

Miss Voise didn't suggest they call her Esther, but her manner was friendly enough. She led them into her living room and gestured them toward the couch.

"It's been so long since anyone's asked me about the murder," she said as they all sat down. "But I remember that day as if it were yesterday. The street was jam-packed with police cars, and there were so many people going in and out of Dr. Niebuhr's house, it needed a revolving door."

Cole smiled at the remark, then opened his briefcase.

Beth's pulse began racing as he pulled out the folder with the snapshot inside.

"It's not actually the murder that we want to ask about," he said. "We'd like to know if you recall ever seeing this man visiting the Niebuhrs' house."

Beth held her breath while Cole flipped open the folder and handed Esther the picture.

She looked at it for a couple of seconds, then said, "Oh, yes, I certainly do."

Her words made Beth feel as if someone had punched her impossibly hard, and such a loud pounding started in her ears that she could barely hear the rest of what the woman was saying.

"I remember seeing him many times," she continued. "That's a picture of the brother-in-law. Larisa's sister's husband."

The pounding began to fade. Her father hadn't

been the mystery man. Weak with relief, she tuned back in to what Esther Voise was saying.

"They'd come over for barbecues the odd time during the summer. And they'd always bring their little girl—the poor little thing who was there when Larisa was murdered. You know about her, I imagine."

Cole nodded.

"The poor little thing," Esther said again. "She was so traumatized by the murder that she could never remember whether she'd seen it."

"Oh?" Cole said. "That wasn't in the newspapers, was it?"

"No, but you know how neighbors find out about things. And the papers never get things right anyway. They said she was off playing in the basement, which just couldn't have been true. She'd have been wherever Larisa was. Larisa positively doted on her.

"But why did you ask me about the brother-in-law?" Esther asked, abruptly switching topics and looking at the snapshot once more.

Cole tried to think of a logical answer. He hadn't been expecting this turn of events, hadn't thought about the Gregorys socializing as a couple—not after Niebuhr had talked about them leading separate lives. But the possibility should have at least crossed his mind.

Mentally kicking himself, he said, "A bit of new information's come to light."

Esther nodded. "Yes, you told me that when you phoned."

"A few photographs," he said, hoping he sounded believable. "And we didn't know who this man was."

"But Mark Niebuhr could have told you," Esther pointed out, looking suspicious. "And you said you were working for him."

"Yes, we are." Quickly, Cole produced Niebuhr's card and showed it to her. "But we haven't met with Dr. Niebuhr since we were given the photos. And we wanted to talk to you, anyway, so we thought we'd show you the picture while we were here," he added, breathing more easily when her suspicious expression faded.

"Oh. Oh, yes, I guess I misunderstood. I thought you'd come specifically to show me the picture. What did you really want to talk to me about, then?"

"The man you told the police about—the one they were never able to identify."

"The one with the ponytail."

"Yes."

"Oh, you can't know how much I wished I'd been able to describe him better. Not that I saw him the day of the murder or anything, but I knew they'd have liked to question him about it. I'd only seen him three times, though. And I'd never really gotten much of a look at him.

"The first time, he was standing on the front steps before I noticed him. That was in early spring—late March or the beginning of April was what I recalled at the time."

"And he used the front door?"

"Yes, they all did." She hesitated, then added, "You do know that Larisa used to entertain a lot of...friends."

"Yes, I think we have most of that story."

"Well, I was never as judgmental about it as some people. And I wasn't the neighborhood busybody, either. I didn't stand around watching what was going on. I was a nurse, so I led a busy life of my own. But with my shift work, I was quite often at home during the day. And I'd just sometimes happen to look out the window and see one of them coming or going."

"Of course."

"At any rate, the first time I saw this one, I thought to myself, that's one I haven't seen before. The ponytail made me realize that. He was wearing a baseball cap, and his ponytail was hanging through the hole in the back. Brown," she added. "He had brown hair."

"And the other times you saw him? Did you notice anything more?"

"Nothing very helpful, I'm afraid. As I told the police, he was average height, average weight, and I guessed somewhere in his thirties. The only other thing was that every time I saw him he was wearing a hat.

"The second time, it was one of those off-white canvas things with a brim. And the last time, it was a brown leather one—kind of a Mexican cowboy hat, it looked like. I remember thinking how hot his head must have been, and wondering why anyone would wear a leather hat in July."

"July," Cole repeated. "So the last time you saw him wasn't long before the murder."

"No, only a week or so."

"And you never had a feeling there was anything familiar about him? He couldn't have been someone you'd ever seen other times? Maybe not wearing a hat?"

When Esther hesitated, Cole glanced at Beth. She

was watching the older woman closely, her expression tense.

For her sake, he hoped Esther Voise was positive the man with the ponytail had been a total stranger to her.

On the other hand, if Glen Gregory was the murderer, the sooner they came up with some hard evidence of that, the better. And if he wasn't guilty, why the hell would he have been tailing them?

"I don't think there was anything familiar about him," Esther said at last. "I know nothing struck me at the time. But since I never got much more than a glimpse of him, I suppose it's possible."

"And what about Larisa's other visitors?" Cole said. "Did you see much of them in the weeks before the murder?"

"No. In fact, I didn't remember seeing any of them at all. But as I said, I wasn't just standing around watching."

AFTER SHE AND COLE said their goodbyes to Esther Voise, Beth didn't utter another word. She knew exactly why Cole had asked whether there'd been anything familiar about the mystery man, and she simply wasn't up to talking about it.

Frank Abbot had said the ponytail could have been fake. Which meant there was a chance Esther *had* seen the man other times. Looking different. Possibly looking like Mark and Larisa's brother-in-law. *That* was what Cole had been fishing for.

She bit her lower lip, morosely aware that she wasn't nearly as convinced of her father's innocence as she'd initially been.

Immediately after she'd recalled the murder, she'd

had only the tiniest fear that he might really have been the killer. But the fear had been growing. And the fact that it had, the fact that she could seriously suspect her own father of something so monstrous, was eating her up inside. They were back in the Mustang and pulling away from the curb before she forced herself to speak.

"Cole? If Esther Voise had ever seen the mystery man in a different context, don't you think she'd have sensed there was something familiar about him?"

"She might have. But don't forget she only caught glimpses of him each time."

"Well, they were long enough glimpses that she knew he was the same man."

"Beth," he said gently, "a ponytail's kind of hard to miss, even with just a glimpse."

"But she said she'd seen my father *many* times. So surely there'd have been something. The way he walked, or…something."

Cole simply reached across and rested his hand on hers, as if he could feel her frustration.

"Look," he said, pulling up at the stop sign when they reached Avenue Road. "We went in there thinking she might say your father was the mystery man, but she didn't. That's the good news. The not-so-good news is that we're dealing with what was probably a disguise, so…we'll just keep on digging until we learn what we need to."

He didn't move his hand from hers when he'd finished speaking, and his touch helped—but not nearly enough.

Esther Voise had never even suspected that Glen Gregory was the mystery man, let alone recognized him as Larisa's unidentified visitor. That should have been enough to clear him.

But because of a stupid ponytail and some hats, it wasn't. And that just wasn't fair.

BETH LOOKED UP FROM the magazine article she couldn't make herself concentrate on and glanced over at Cole.

Normally, she'd hate spending a nice summer evening cooped up in her apartment with nothing except reruns on television. But under the current circumstances, she was only too happy to be right here where she felt relatively safe, listening to Mariah Carey's latest CD and reading.

She turned her attention back to the article and made it through a few more sentences. Before long, though, she found herself looking at Cole again— and trying not to wish he was sitting on the couch beside her rather than in a chair.

Of course, he would be if she'd given him the slightest encouragement. She was sure of that. But she'd effectively discouraged him, because she still hadn't finished trying to sort through her feelings in the Brian/Cole department. And until she had...

She eyed him for another few moments, thinking he looked so very right sitting there. Then she remembered that was exactly what she'd thought when he'd been sitting in the kitchen with her, eating the pizza they'd picked up on their way back from Esther Voise's.

In any event, at the moment she couldn't imagine how he could possibly look more right. He was reading a murder mystery, with Bogey contentedly purring on his lap and Bacall draped over the back of his chair, one of her front paws lightly resting on his shoulder.

Brian, she absently reflected, didn't like the cats "groveling around him," as he put it. But why was she thinking about that? Was she mentally building a case for ending things with Brian?

A *case*. As the word began to drift around in her mind, her thoughts turned to the real case. Cole had said there wasn't much work they could do on it tonight, but she wished there had been.

Actually, what she wished was that they'd already learned who'd killed her aunt. And who was targeting her. Because the uncertainty—not to mention the little matter of her life being in danger—had her nerves completely on edge.

"You know what I've been wondering about?" Cole asked, looking up from his book.

She smiled, forcing away her thoughts of uncertainty and danger. "Do I look like a mind reader?"

"Very funny. But be serious and listen. There's something bothering me about your uncle."

"Oh? What?"

"Well, I can't help thinking that if the average guy's wife was murdered, and afterward he found out she'd been as unfaithful as Larisa was... You know what I'm trying to say? Don't you think his memory of her would be tarnished, to say the least?"

"I...yes, that certainly makes sense."

"Then why does your uncle seem so...almost obsessed with her memory? I mean, there's this ritual with the three of you going to the cemetery every year, and—"

"A lot of families do that sort of thing."

"I know they do. Oh, and by the way, I'll be going with you tomorrow."

"I'm not sure Mark would like that. My mother might not, either. Because I guess you're right, it is a ritual."

And it was kind of a morbid one, although she didn't admit that. She simply added, "We do everything the same way each year. Larisa was murdered sometime after ten in the morning, so we always meet there before ten."

"Why?"

She shook her head. "That's just the way Mark wants it. And afterward, we go back to my mother's house for lunch. Just the three of us. It's always been like that. Even the first year, when my parents were still together, they didn't ask my father to join us."

"Well, they'll just have to cope with someone joining them this year."

Beth didn't offer any further objection. Regardless of what the others would like, she'd feel a whole lot better with Cole there.

"At any rate," he continued, "getting back to your uncle and Larisa—when you finally remembered witnessing the murder, why was Mark so adamant about following up on it right away? Even though he admitted you could have remembered the wrong face? I mean, after twenty-two years, why was he pressuring you to go to the police immediately? And when you refused, why did he drag you to see me the very next day? Hell, you should have been home in bed. You looked like a zombie."

"Thank you very much," she said, softening the sarcasm with a smile.

When Cole quietly said, "An extremely pretty

zombie,'' the words started a slow ripple of heat through her.

"Just one who should have been resting up,'' he added, "instead of being in my office. But the point is, what difference would a few days have made?''

"Well,'' she said slowly, thinking it should have occurred to her to wonder why Mark had been so determined to rush into this. But she had been a zombie, and she hadn't been thinking clearly about anything.

"I guess he didn't want to wait because that's just the way he is,'' she continued at last. "When he makes a decision, he acts on it right away.''

Before Cole said anything more, the phone began to ring. He glanced at it, then at her.

When she didn't move, he lifted Bogey off his lap and pushed himself out of the chair.

"You think this is your caller, don't you?'' he asked, looking at the caller ID display. It was reading Caller Unknown.

"It might be. He usually phones at night.''

Cole picked up the cordless, clicked it on and packed his hello with menace.

"Yeah, she's here,'' he added a moment later, handing her the phone, then heading back to his chair.

It was Brian, and his first words were "Who was that?''

She swore to herself. She didn't want to try filling him in via long distance. "It's a complicated story,'' she said. "I'll tell you about it when you get back.''

"Beth, if you were three thousand miles away, and a strange woman answered my phone, wouldn't you be curious?''

"Yes, of course. But…oh, all right. I've started to

remember Larisa's murder. And because I have, Mark hired a private investigator. That's who answered the phone. We were in the midst of discussing the case."

"The case?" Brian said. "What case?"

"I just told you. Mark's hired an investigator to look into Larisa's murder, and—"

"After all these years? And this guy's in your apartment in the middle of the night discussing it with you?"

"It's hardly the middle of the night."

"Maybe not, but you were eight years old when your aunt was murdered. What the hell information can you give him about the *case?*"

The sarcasm in Brian's voice started anger simmering inside her. Anger mixed with...resentment? And with annoyance that he always seemed to think he could be running her life better than she was?

Usually, she simply ignored that, but—for whatever reason—it really irked her tonight.

"Actually," she said cooly, "I'm not giving him information. I'm working on the investigation with him."

"Get outta here! You're not serious."

"Yes. I am."

Brian muttered something she didn't catch, then said, "You know, when we met, I thought you were this great, uncomplicated woman who really had it together. But for the last couple of months... And now what? You've decided to play V. I. Warshawski?

"Beth, maybe you can't see it from the inside looking out, but you haven't exactly been the easiest person to get along with lately. Have you been trying to give me a message, or what?''

"No, I haven't.'' She glanced uneasily at Cole, not wanting to get dragged into a conversation like this with him sitting there listening.

"No? Well it's sure been seeming that way to me. Every time we talk about moving in together, I end up thinking it's never going to happen. And for the past hour I've been sitting here in this hotel room by myself, thinking about that and... And I think maybe it's decision time. Here and now.''

She took a deep, slow breath, not sure if she was making the decision right this moment or if she'd subconsciously made it earlier.

"I still don't feel ready,'' she said at last. As she spoke, she waited for the dreadful pain that was sure to come.

It didn't. She felt shaky, strangely hollow inside, and not far from tears, but there was no intolerable, overwhelming pain of loss.

After a long silence, Brian slowly said, "Okay, I guess I'm not really surprised. So let's not see each other for a while, okay?''

The hollow feeling began to grow, and the silence lengthened while she tried to think of what else she should say.

It seemed they'd said too little for people who'd been seeing each other for months, and she couldn't help wondering if she'd come to regret this. But she couldn't think of anything more to say right now.

Finally, Brian cleared his throat and said, "Before we hang up, will you be talking to your father in the next day or two?''

"My father?''

"Yeah, I called him the other day and suggested a round of golf on the weekend. He seemed to enjoy playing last month."

"Aah…right, he did," she lied. The first time Brian had invited him, her father had only gone out of politeness. And she knew he hadn't enjoyed himself.

"Well, if you're talking to him, mention that something's come up and I won't be able to make it, okay?"

"All right. I will."

"And…take care of yourself."

"You, too," she said, still not quite able to believe they were both managing to be so civil and unemotional. Did that mean whatever there'd been between them had gradually faded away without them noticing?

She wondered about that for a few seconds, then realized something else was nagging at her. She wasn't sure what it was, but just as Brian was saying goodbye, her mind zoomed in on it.

For a frozen second, she couldn't make herself speak. Then she said, "Wait. Wait, there's something I have to ask you. When you were golfing with my father last month, did you happen to mention that I was trying to make myself remember Larisa's murder?"

Cole sat up straighter in his chair.

Bogey meowed a complaint about being disturbed.

Beth held her breath, waiting for Brian's reply.

Chapter Ten

Slowly, Beth put down the cordless and looked at Cole. He'd moved over to the couch, and he was sitting close enough that she could smell the woodsy scent of his aftershave and see the concern in his eyes.

"Your father knew," he said quietly.

She nodded. "For the past month. Brian just assumed I'd mentioned it to him, and made some remark about wishing Mark and I would leave well enough alone. Then, when my father didn't know what he was talking about, he had to explain.

"But when I told my father I'd started to remember..."

"He acted as if it was the first he was hearing about any of it."

"Why?" she whispered, staring down at the couch and telling herself there must be several possible answers—and that, among them, there was at least one that wouldn't make her father appear even more guilty.

"Beth? Let's stop talking about it for a bit, okay? You just finished one hell of a conversation. And, look, I'm sorry you didn't have privacy for it. I'd have gone for a walk or something if I'd realized what was coming.''

She shrugged unhappily.

''Is there anything I can do? Or do you want to talk about it?''

''No, it… It's been coming for a while, I guess. He's been trying to convince me to live with him and I just didn't feel right about it and… Well, it doesn't matter.''

Cole rubbed his jaw, eyeing her intently.

''What?'' she finally said.

''How was he trying to convince you?''

She shrugged again. ''He just kept bringing it up. Telling me it was a good idea. That he hated the thought of me waking up to the nightmares alone. That a woman shouldn't be living on her own in a neighborhood like this.''

''You don't think… Look, is there any chance he's been your crank caller? Trying to make you afraid to be on your own?''

That thought was enough to send a shiver through her. But it couldn't have been him. ''No. He's basically a nice guy.''

''Even nice guys can do some pretty crazy things when it comes to women. Have you ever had one of the calls while he's been here?''

''No,'' she said uneasily. ''But I just can't believe…''

''Okay. I guess I shouldn't even be asking about it right now. Sometimes, I have the world's worst sense of timing. So, look, why don't you just try to relax. Try to make your mind go blank and give yourself a time-out.''

When she met his gaze, he looked as if he cared

very much about her well-being—far more than he realistically could, considering how briefly they'd known each other.

It made her feel like crying because, absurd as it might be, she wanted him to care that much.

"Oh, Cole," she murmured. "Everything is just so awful right now."

For a fraction of a second more, he simply looked at her. Then he draped his arms around her and pulled her to him.

Closing her eyes, she snuggled against him, feeling as if she'd found a safe haven in a storm. The solid warmth of his body was comforting, the steady thudding of his heart was reassuring.

She loved the way being close to him made her feel. Loved his gentle touch, his scent, his warmth, and the lean hardness of his body against hers.

As he stroked her hair, his body heat gradually began spreading through her—slow and sweet as spilled honey—and an ache of desire started low in her belly.

That told her she'd done exactly what she should have as far as Brian was concerned. She might have been a little slow at being certain of it, but he couldn't possibly have been the right man for her. Not when she could feel this way in another man's arms.

"You okay?" Cole whispered against her hair.

She looked at him—her gaze drifting over the square line of his jaw, lingering on his broad, sensual mouth, moving on to those little laugh lines, finally coming to rest when it reached the hazel warmth of his eyes.

"Not exactly," she murmured. "As my mother would say, I'm feeling a little fragile."

He slowly smoothed his thumb across her cheek, then trailed his fingers down her neck, sending little shivers of delight through her.

"I'd never want to take advantage of anyone's fragility," he said softly. "Especially not yours."

His breath was a warm, whispering breeze against her skin. His mouth was mere inches from hers. His eyes were saying he *wouldn't* take advantage of her, that the next move was hers.

Gazing at him, she thought how totally out of character it would be for her to get involved with him when she'd barely ended another relationship.

But that slow, spilled-honey feeling inside her kept growing warmer, and the longer she looked at him the harder it became to resist him—and the less desire she had to.

Finally, she leaned forward those mere inches, cradled his head in her hands and parted her lips to his.

He tasted her and she tasted back, slowly and lazily at first, then more and more hungrily, until the heat curling through her veins began to sizzle and that ache of desire was almost too strong to bear.

They kissed until it was too much and not enough, until finally, breathlessly, she forced her lips from his and rested her cheek against his shoulder.

"Somehow," she whispered, gazing at him, "I don't think that's in your job description."

When he smiled, it lit up his face. She'd noticed long ago how engaging his smile was. But she hadn't realized until now that it was positively the nicest one she'd ever seen.

"It's worse than just not being part of my job

description," he said. "I've got a rule about not mixing business with pleasure."

"Oh? And you never break the rules?"

"Only under very unusual circumstances."

"Like...?"

"Like when I come across a lady who's downright irresistible."

"And does that happen very often?"

He smiled again, slowly shaking his head. "First time ever."

His words made her feel flushed and...giddy. Such an old-fashioned word, yet it perfectly described the way she was feeling—as if there were so many champagne bubbles inside her that they were about to start spilling out in a fit of giggles.

"Feeling better?" he asked.

"Definitely," she told him. "Maybe even good enough to talk about my father."

"I've got another idea, if you're up to it."

"What's that?"

"Talk *to* him."

COLE SANK DOWN BESIDE Beth, every nerve ending in his body aware that they were sitting on the edge of her bed. Then she slid the bedside phone closer to her, and he reminded himself they were only in the bedroom so they'd have both that phone and the cordless.

But he could easily picture them here for an entirely different reason. And just thinking about it was making him hard with arousal.

He could still taste the sweetness of her kisses, could still feel the softness of her body. And it was awfully difficult not to imagine himself making love with her. But no matter what, he wasn't going to make a serious move on her tonight.

In the space of mere minutes, she'd broken up with her boyfriend and learned her father had lied to her. And even if it was merely a lie of omission, it was another nail in the coffin of his guilt. So coming on to her tonight...

Hell, he'd spend until morning in a cold shower before he'd let himself do that.

"This just doesn't seem right," she said, reaching to pick up the receiver, then hesitating. "Somehow, my telling you what he said afterward wouldn't be as bad as your listening in. That's downright spying."

"Anyone ever tell you you've got an overdeveloped sense of fair play?"

When that didn't make her smile, he took her hand and gave it a reassuring squeeze.

Considering the state she was in, he didn't want to push her any harder than he had to. But if her father had known all along that she was trying to make that memory surface, then the idea of his driving around with coveralls and a gorilla mask in his trunk—just waiting for his chance—wasn't at all far-fetched.

"Hey, I'm the pro here, remember," he coaxed. "And I need to know exactly what he says and how he says it."

Not looking the least bit happier, she punched in the number. When she nodded that it was ringing, Cole clicked on the cordless and put it to his ear.

After the third ring, Glen Gregory picked up.

Cole took Beth's hand again, hoping to hell she could manage this.

"It's me, Dad," she said, keeping her eyes on Cole and sounding only a little nervous.

He nodded, shooting her one of the "reassuring" looks they'd taught him at cop school.

"Well, hi," Gregory said.

"I…was just talking to Brian and he asked me to phone you for him."

"Oh?" Gregory's tone cooled a degree or two—not surprising when Beth had mentioned that Brian wasn't one of his favorite people.

"He had to go to Vancouver on business, and he's not sure he'll be back for the weekend. So he wanted me to tell you, because you had a golf date or something?"

Cole gave her an encouraging smile. So far, she wasn't doing badly.

"Oh, that was only tentative," Gregory said. "But thanks for letting me know."

Beth hesitated, her anxiety almost palpable. "No problem. I wanted to talk to you about something else, anyway." She was squeezing Cole's hand now, harder than he'd have believed she was capable of.

"What's that?" Gregory asked.

"Well, when I was talking to Brian…"

You're doing fine, Cole mouthed.

"He happened to mention that he told you I was trying to remember witnessing the murder. When the two of you were golfing last month, he said it was.

"So I was wondering, when I told you I had started to remember bits about it…why didn't you say you knew I'd been trying to?"

"Aah," Gregory said, stretching out the sound. "Yes, I thought at the time that maybe I should."

"Then why didn't you?"

"Well…you said I was the first person you'd told—aside from Mark and that detective. And it…this is probably going to sound silly, but it pleased me. I mean, I haven't been the first person you've told about *anything* since you were a little girl. And it felt…almost as if you were giving me a present. So I didn't want to spoil the moment."

"Oh." Beth looked uncertainly at Cole.

He shrugged. Gregory's explanation was certainly plausible.

"If I'd known Brian was going to fill you in," he added, "I'd have said something. But I figured that if he hadn't mentioned he'd told me by that point, he'd forgotten all about it."

"Oh," Beth said again.

The car, Cole mouthed.

She scrunched up her face in an "I don't want to" expression, but said, "By the way, I thought I saw you today. Around four-thirty or so? Driving behind Cole and me? Along Bloor and then up Bedford?"

"No, it wasn't me. I was in my office until almost six."

"Oh…it looked like your car. But I guess it couldn't have been, then."

"Not unless somebody took it for a joyride," he said with a quiet laugh.

After a few final pleasantries, Beth said goodbye and hung up, looking as if she were about to start crying any second.

"Oh, Cole," she whispered, "he just can't be a murderer. Did you hear what he said? That when I told him, he felt as if I was giving him a present?

"That's so sad. All those years when I almost never saw him, I thought he didn't care about me.

But he must have been thinking that *I* didn't care about *him*. I mean, if simply telling him something before I told anyone else..."

When she wiped away a tear that had spilled over, Cole felt such a strong urge to take her in his arms that he could barely resist. But he made himself do with merely brushing a few stray hairs back from her cheek.

"You've had one hell of a long day," he said gently. "Why don't you turn in and get some sleep."

She sat gazing at him, the sadness in her eyes making him think she could do with the comfort of a warm body. But there was no way on earth he'd be able to stop at merely comforting her.

"See you in the morning," he said, giving her a kiss on the cheek, then forcing himself to stand up and walk out of the room.

AFTER HE LEFT BETH in her bedroom, Cole switched on the TV, knowing there was no way he'd get to sleep for hours. His mind was too busy with thoughts of how wonderful she felt in his arms. And with a hundred and one questions he wanted answers to.

They played on his mind while he watched the eleven o'clock news, then Letterman, and finally a crummy movie.

Was her own father really trying to kill her? And if not, who was? And what about this creep who'd been calling her? Was it Brian? Without knowing the guy, it was hard to even make a good guess.

When his eyelids finally started feeling heavy, he switched off the TV and made up his bed on the couch. Then, just as he was about to undress, he heard a quiet noise in the hallway.

Grabbing his gun, he quickly headed into Beth's office and peered through the peephole—in time to see the door of Marlon Birch's apartment closing.

Thinking that the hours musicians kept were brutal, he tucked his gun against the small of his back, turned away from the door and stood gazing down at the night street.

All was still. Until the phone began to ring.

Wheeling around, he peered through the darkness at the caller ID display. It was reading Caller Unknown. He dashed for the bedroom.

By the time he got there, Beth had the bedside light on and was sitting up in bed, staring at the phone.

"Answer it," he told her. "And if it's him, keep him on the line."

Looking incredibly anxious, she picked up the receiver and said, "Hello?"

When she nodded to him, he took off. Pausing only to get a glass from the kitchen, he raced through her office and out into the hallway. Then he crossed quietly to Birch's door and pressed the glass to the wood.

It was hardly high-tech, but it worked. Birch's words were faint but audible.

"I just had a feeling you'd like to hear from me tonight," he was saying. "I've been thinking we should get together. Meet face-to-face. No? You don't think so? Well, maybe I should surprise you. Maybe, sometime when you're all alone someplace, I'll just come up and introduce myself. 'Cuz I think you and me'd have a real good time."

Adrenaline and anger surging through him, Cole dropped the glass and karate-kicked the door open.

Birch wheeled around and stood staring at him—a cellular in his hand that had an attachment over the mouthpiece. Undoubtedly, that's what was altering his voice.

After an initial startled second, he tossed the phone onto the couch and snarled, "What the hell do you think you're doing?"

"I'll give you a hint." Cole pulled the gun from his waistband and aimed it at the creep.

His face paled. "Wait a minute. I don't know what you're thinking, but you've got something real wrong here."

Cole clicked off the safety, then worked the slide. Birch swallowed hard and rubbed his palms against his jeans.

"Look," he tried again, sweat appearing on his forehead. "Whatever you're thinking is wrong."

Before Cole could reply, Beth came hurrying into the apartment—still tugging on her robe.

"You're just in time," he told her. "Your friend here's about to tell me why he's been playing games with you."

"I..."

"Spit it out!" Cole menacingly waved his gun.

"I...I was just trying to take her down a peg or two. She figured she was too damn good for me, and I was just giving her a little payback."

"Yeah? Well, guess what? The cops are going to give *you* a little payback. Call them, Beth. Then we'll just wait right here until they arrive."

"IT'S HARDLY WORTH GOING back to bed," Beth said, after the police officers had taken Marlon away.

Cole gave her a tired smile. "One of us hasn't

even been to bed yet, so even a couple of hours sounds good.''

She gazed at him, wishing he'd take her in his arms, even though she knew it was a dangerous wish.

When he didn't, she said, ''Well then, I guess I'll… Cole, I don't know how to thank you.''

''Hey, I was just doing my job. So now there's one mystery solved and only one to go.'' Giving her a gentle kiss on the forehead, he shooed her off to her bedroom.

She closed the door, then climbed into bed again, wishing the ''one to go'' wasn't such an awfully big one. But at least she didn't have to be afraid to answer her phone anymore. And at least her caller hadn't been Brian. If it had turned out she was that bad a judge of character…

Of course, she'd never have figured Marlon was the one, either. Letting him know she wasn't interested—even if she had done it in no uncertain terms—hardly seemed enough provocation for him to have been tormenting her for weeks.

Telling herself you never knew how warped people might be, she tried to make her mind go blank. Gradually, she drifted off into the oblivion of sleep.

And then she came awake with a start, drenched in sweat, her heart pounding.

The cats were on the floor, meowing and staring up at her instead of sleeping at the bottom of the bed, which meant she must have been moving in her sleep.

But that was hardly surprising. She'd been having a doozy of a nightmare—a different one this time, but in its own way just as horrific as the attic one.

In tonight's, she'd been standing beside Cole,

watching her father being strapped into an electric chair.

Sitting up, she turned on the bedside lamp and told herself that could never happen. Canada had abolished the death penalty decades ago. Still, how would she feel if she helped convict him of murder? She exhaled slowly, wishing once again that she'd done more thinking before insisting on being involved in this. But now, as Cole had said, she was in too far to back out.

Yet with more and more things pointing in the direction of her father's guilt... And if he was the murderer, he'd undoubtedly been the gorilla man.

She tried to imagine what learning he'd definitely been the shooter would do to her. And how it would make her feel about Cole, for finding the proof. But that wasn't something she wanted to think about.

She and Cole... It was as if the most unexpected thing had happened at the most unlikely time. And kissing him made her feel as if she'd found something she'd never even known was missing from her life.

But what if they did turn up evidence that helped convict her father? Wouldn't she remember, every time she looked at Cole, that they'd sent her father to jail for the rest of his life?

Of course she would. Because, regardless of what he might have done, he'd still be her father.

And didn't that mean she should put what was happening between her and Cole on hold? Until her life was no longer in danger and they knew for certain if her father was guilty?

Yes, that was undoubtedly the only sensible option. It might not be what she wanted, but anything else would be playing emotional Russian roulette.

Switching off the light, she lay back down and stared up through the skylight, unable to keep from thinking about Cole. She pictured him sitting in her kitchen, eating pizza. And in her living room, reading his book with the cats draped around him.

At the time, he'd seemed so right in those pictures. But how right would he seem if the two of them had destroyed her father?

She lay awake, her thoughts spinning, until the timer on the louvered blind started sliding it silently shut over the skylight, telling her it was almost dawn.

The next thing she knew, Bogey and Bacall were demanding to be let out of the bedroom.

"Just give me two seconds," she told them, climbing out of bed and heading for the tiny en suite bathroom.

She freshened up a little, so she didn't look morning-dreadful, then ran her fingers through her hair and shook it more or less into place. Grabbing her robe and tugging it on, she told herself the very first thing she was going to do was talk to Cole about cooling things between them—for the time being, at least.

After all, she'd been the one who'd initiated the kissing last night. So if she simply tried to keep him at arm's length, without explaining why, he'd figure she'd switched places with an evil twin.

It wasn't until she was heading for the bedroom door that she remembered this was the anniversary of Larisa's death—and began dreading the visit to the cemetery.

They'd put flowers on the grave, the way they always did. Then they'd stand gazing at it, Mark looking as if he were totally lost in memories. Before they were done her mother would end up in tears, the way she always did. And Beth herself...

Normally, she just stood there feeling sad and uncomfortable. But now that she knew Larisa had cheated on Mark, and now that Cole had started her wondering why Mark was obsessed with an unfaithful wife's memory, she'd probably spend the whole visit trying to figure out the reason.

When she opened the bedroom door and followed the cats out, she could smell that Cole had made coffee again this morning. As she neared the kitchen, she could see he'd also put down fresh cat food and made a deli run for bagels and cream cheese.

They were sitting on the counter, looking delicious, while he was sitting on a stool—looking even more delicious.

He was wearing jeans and a blue T-shirt, drinking a mug of the coffee. He hadn't shaved yet, and just like yesterday, his dark growth of beard struck her as outrageously sexy.

Merely looking at him made her want to wrap her arms around him and kiss him good morning. Instead, she slid onto the stool next to his and said, "Mmmm. Someone must have given you lessons on being the perfect houseguest."

He grinned at that, sending a little rush of desire through her.

When he reached for an empty mug and began pouring her coffee, she cleared her throat and ordered herself to start talking. "Cole...about last night?"

He didn't say a word, simply put the mug down in front of her and waited.

She could feel her face growing warm, but this was something she had to do. She delayed the inevitable by taking a couple of sips of coffee, then said, "I guess you couldn't help noticing I find you attractive."

"What a fortunate coincidence." He gave her a killer smile that turned her insides to jelly.

"But…look, I've got a real problem with this whole situation."

His smile faded. "I'm not surprised."

"I mean, between my father looking like our prime suspect and someone shooting at me…"

"And breaking up with Brian," he offered. "And discovering it was your neighbor who's been harassing you."

That took her aback. She hadn't expected him to be helping her out.

Did the fact he was mean he'd been having second thoughts, too? Was he relieved that she wanted to put on the brakes?

Suddenly, her face was well beyond warm. She felt as if it was the color of a tomato.

"Look, Beth," he said quietly, "I'm no Mr. Sensitivity, but I realize your life's not exactly running smoothly at the moment. Hell, saying it's in utter chaos would be more accurate. And I know you must be…well, as my sisters would put it, emotionally vulnerable. So let's get a few other things sorted out before we start dealing with the fact that we're attracted to each other."

She simply stared at him. And the next thing she knew tears were streaming down her face. Never, not in a million years, would she have expected that reaction from a man, and it was so darned sweet she didn't know what she'd do if the other things didn't get sorted out.

Cole sat looking at Beth in disbelief. He never had gotten any sleep. Instead, he'd spent the past couple of hours doing the most rational bit of thinking he'd ever done concerning a woman.

But look at the result. He'd reduced her to tears. So where was the flaw in his thinking? Rapidly, he reviewed it, trying to figure out where he'd gone off track.

It certainly hadn't been in realizing that he was falling for her, because there was no doubt he was. Hell, as fast as it might have happened, he'd already fallen. He wanted her so badly it hurt.

And surely he couldn't be wrong about the emotional vulnerability bit. Not when her life was such a mess. And that meant it would be a big mistake for her to get involved with anyone at the moment.

What she thought she wanted now wasn't necessarily what she'd want once her life was back to normal—assuming it ever got there. And from his point of view, he wasn't crazy about the possibility he'd get left hurting when that time came.

Dammit, all his logic still made perfect sense to him. So what was the problem?

"Beth?" he said at last. "What did I say wrong?"

She shook her head and wiped her eyes. "Nothing. Absolutely nothing. I just… Oh, Cole, this isn't really what I want."

Then what on earth *did* she want?

"I must look like hell," she murmured, wiping her eyes again.

"No, you look fine. Terrific, even. There's something about the red-nosed, tearstained look that I've always found cute.''

"Oh, Cole.'' She managed something that almost looked like a smile. "I don't know what I'd do without you right now.''

He wasn't sure which of them moved, but a second later he was kissing her. She tasted of tears and coffee, a combination he'd never have imagined could taste half as good as it did.

Indulging himself in the warm sweetness of the kiss, he tried not to think about anything except the moment. But he couldn't entirely forget her words.

She'd said, "I don't know what I'd do without you *right now*.'' Which was perfectly in line with what he'd been thinking.

And if what she figured she wanted now turned out to not be what she'd want once this was all over, where would that leave him?

Chapter Eleven

A cemetery would never have been Cole's first choice of destinations on a warm sunny morning like this one. But since that was where Beth had to be, it was where he was going. Besides, not letting her out of his sight wasn't exactly a hardship.

When he glanced across the car, she looked so kissable that his lips began to tingle. He forced his eyes from her and stared straight ahead once more, trying not to think about how sensuous her kisses were.

After their little session in the kitchen, he'd warned himself—yet again—that he was treading in very dangerous waters. But since he could still feel himself getting in deeper and deeper, practically with every breath he took, the warning had obviously done no good.

Ordering himself to think about something other than Beth, he turned his thoughts to her mother. He'd be meeting her when they got to the cemetery, and he was more than a little curious about her.

Even though Glen Gregory was looking like a shoo-in as the murderer, sometimes a killer turned out to be the most unlikely person imaginable. And that time lag between when Angela Gregory had discovered her sister's body and when she'd called the police had bothered him from the beginning.

Not that he figured there was any real chance she was guilty. And he certainly didn't want her to be. Hell, for Beth's sake, he didn't want her father to be, either. But as Mick Jagger had immortalized in song, you can't always get what you want.

Glancing across the car again, he said, "Tell me about your mother."

"My mother?"

"Yeah. I always like to know a little about people before I meet them."

"What sort of a little?"

"Oh, how about starting with where she lives and what she does."

"Well, she still lives in the house I grew up in, near Royal York, just north of Dundas. It's a big two-story place, far too big for one person. But she got it as part of the divorce settlement, and she's never wanted to sell—I think mostly because people have always told her she should."

Cole smiled. "She doesn't take kindly to advice?"

"Mmm...I guess that's a fair way of putting it. She got some money as part of the settlement, too, and she didn't listen to anybody's advice about what to do with it, either. She invested it in a fitness club."

"People invest in fitness clubs?"

"Well, this one's actually more than that. It's a women's club with spa facilities and a first-rate restaurant—plus the regular exercise equipment and pool and everything.

"A lot of the members are pretty high-powered women. At any rate, it was just in the planning stages when my mother got her settlement, and they were actively seeking women investors.''

"Aah. It's a sexist club, then."

Beth smiled. It made him want to kiss her.

"It's also a successful one," she said. "I'm sure, way back when, everyone thought Mom was going to lose her shirt. But she didn't. And since she's been a lifelong fitness nut, she ended up on staff as well as being an investor.

"She's in charge of the exercise classes—everything from scheduling them to hiring the instructors. It doesn't take all her time, but it's enough to keep her busy.

"Oh, no, don't turn here," she said when he flicked on his signal. "The first entrance off Wharton is the closest to Larisa's grave."

Flicking the signal back off, he drove on up the block between Russell and Wharton, thinking about the fact that a lifelong fitness nut would have always been in good shape. And that Abbot had said Larisa Niebuhr could have been murdered by a woman.

Telling himself his imagination was getting way out of line, he turned into the cemetery's entrance and followed Beth's directions to the grave.

"It's where those two cars are parked up ahead," she said, anxiously glancing at her watch. "That's my mom talking to Mark."

"We're not late," Cole assured her, pulling up behind the other cars. The white Cadillac had personalized plates that read MN MD. Which meant that the green Taurus parked ahead of it had to be Angela Gregory's.

"Wait a sec," he told Beth as she reached for her

door handle. Taking a slow look around, he satisfied himself that there was nobody else in sight.

"What?" she said nervously. "You think our gorilla man might be lurking behind a tombstone?"

"It's pretty unlikely in broad daylight, but there's no sense taking chances."

"Does that mean you're wearing your gun?"

He pushed his suit jacket aside far enough that she could see his holster, then reached past her and opened the passenger's door. Canada's gun laws were strict, and he really shouldn't be carrying, but under the circumstances, obeying the letter of the law didn't strike him as the wisest thing to do.

While Beth headed over to her mother and uncle, hugging each of them in turn, Cole climbed out of the Mustang and assessed things.

Larisa's grave was marked by an impressive marble headstone, its inscription carved in letters large enough to be read from the road. There was a white marble dove perched on either corner, and two large flower urns stood at ground level.

It made him wonder once again why Niebuhr seemed to hold Larisa's memory in such high esteem. Was it his way of denying that she'd been a less than perfect wife?

Telling himself he wasn't the psychiatrist, Cole focused on Angela Gregory. In her early fifties, she was an older version of Beth—about five foot six or seven, slim, with blond hair.

The killer, he could hear Abbot saying in his imagination, *was right-handed and somewhere between about five foot seven and five-eleven.*

Angela Gregory, he noted, was wearing her watch

on her left wrist, which likely meant she was right-handed.

"Cole," Niebuhr said, stepping toward him. "I didn't expect to see you here."

Cole shook the man's hand, thinking he didn't need to be a detective to realize that neither the good doctor nor Angela Gregory were pleased to see him.

"Mom," Beth said, "this is Cole Radford."

"Yes, so I gather." Angela gave him a brittle smile.

"I invited him to come back to the house for lunch, too," Beth added.

"Oh. How nice."

When Beth shot him an uneasy glance, Cole said, "If I'll be in the way, Mrs. Gregory…"

"No. No, of course not. I have lots of food. And, please, call me Angela."

As she was speaking, Niebuhr walked over to the Caddy, opened the back door and took out three bunches of roses—two red and one white.

While Cole was trying to figure out if there was any symbolism in that, Niebuhr handed one bunch to Beth and one to her mother. Then, in turn, the three of them walked to the grave and silently placed the flowers—Beth and her mother putting the red ones in the urns, Niebuhr laying the white ones on the grave.

After that, they all backed off and stood gazing downward. It gave Cole an eerie feeling, and he wondered how it made Beth feel. But he didn't have much time to wonder before he heard a car coming down the road.

Turning, he focused on it. A dark blue Chevy, it was traveling at an appropriately slow pace for a cemetery, but with the glare of the sunlight on the windshield, it was impossible to see the driver's face.

Not taking his eyes off the car, Cole moved to Beth's side.

"You think it's trouble?" she murmured.

"Probably not," he whispered, but his gut was telling him he shouldn't be too sure about that.

The Chevy slowly passed his Mustang, the Cadillac, then the Taurus. A second after it emerged from behind the three parked cars, he saw a flash of silver and shots were splitting the air.

"Get down!" he yelled, grabbing for his gun with one hand and dragging Beth down with the other.

Shielding her with his body, he began firing. The Chevy surged forward, its wheels screaming against the pavement as it raced down the road.

Cole shoved himself up, hoping to catch a look at the license, but the car had already rounded a curve and was gone. He took a full cartridge clip from his pocket and replaced the spent one with it, just in case.

When he turned toward the others, they were all still on the ground. Niebuhr and Angela were as white as sheets. Beth was visibly trembling. Behind her, one of the marble doves had been shot off Larisa's gravestone.

His heart still pounding, he helped Beth up and wrapped his arm around her.

"Are you okay?" he asked the other two as they got to their feet.

"Yes," Angela whispered. "But thank heavens you had a gun. If you hadn't shot back he might not have taken off so fast."

"Yes. Thank heavens," Niebuhr said, brushing dirt off his suit.

Holstering his gun, Cole said, "I've got a phone in my car. I'll go call the police."

"Wait," Beth said. "Wait. Just give me one minute."

She picked up her purse from where it had fallen, then dug her cellular out and punched in a number.

"Mr. Gregory, please," she said after a few seconds. "It's his daughter calling." She didn't sound like herself, and she looked scared half to death.

Cole glanced at Niebuhr and Angela. He looked tense. She looked both frightened and puzzled.

Then relief flooded Beth's face and she said, "Dad, I wasn't sure you'd be there." She sounded almost normal again.

"What on earth are you doing?" Angela whispered loudly. "We just about got killed and you're making a social call to your father?"

It took only a quick look at Niebuhr to establish that he knew exactly what Beth was doing.

Then Cole looked at her again, and her expression told him she didn't know what to say to her father now that she'd reached him—that she hadn't thought past square one.

It had been a hell of a good square one, though. He'd give her credit for that.

"I guess," he said, ostensibly to Angela, "she just wants to let him know she's all right. A drive-by shooting in Toronto the Good will be the top news story of the day, and you know how the media loves to sensationalize things."

Beth gave him a look of such utter gratitude he almost smiled.

"But she has to call him right now?" Angela demanded. "Before you even call the police?"

Nobody replied to her questions. Beth was already walking away from them and quietly talking to her father, while Niebuhr picked up on what Cole had said.

"A drive-by shooting? You really think that's all it was?"

"What else would it have been?" Angela said.

Cole eyed Niebuhr evenly, waiting to see which way the good doctor was going to jump.

Finally, he shrugged. "Nothing, I guess. I don't know why anybody would want to intentionally shoot at one of us."

That wasn't true, Cole knew. But the man Niebuhr suspected might have a reason couldn't have been in that car. Because he was sitting in his office, talking on the phone to Beth.

AFTER HER FATHER SAID goodbye and hung up, Beth kept the phone to her ear and pretended she was still in the midst of their conversation.

Cole was standing beside the Mustang, talking on his phone to the police, and she wanted a quick strategy meeting with him before she had to face her mother and uncle.

She knew he didn't really believe it had been a drive-by shooting. He figured exactly what she did. The man in that car had to have been their gorilla man from the other night. And she'd just established it wasn't her father.

Her pulse did a funny little dance as she let herself relish that fact once more. She'd been right to doubt her memory and wrong to doubt her father. He wasn't the one trying to kill her. It was whoever had really murdered her aunt.

Finally, Cole stuck his phone into the pocket of his suit jacket.

"Bye, then," she said into her phone, starting rapidly toward him.

When he saw her coming he stopped walking. "The cops who arrive are going to know we got shot at the other night," he said as she reached him.

"What?"

"I told them this was the second incident."

"Oh, I wish you hadn't. My mother's going to have a fit when she hears that. Mark, too."

"Well, it was the only thing I could do. There's a record of my calling in the first one, and this is the computer age. They'd have matched up the two in no time. And if I hadn't volunteered the information, they'd have wondered why the hell I didn't."

"So they'll know this wasn't any drive-by. They'll know somebody's after me."

"They'll know somebody's after one of us. I was with you both times."

"Beth?" her mother called.

"We'll just be a minute," she called back. "We don't have to tell the police about my memory surfacing, do we?" she asked Cole.

"At this point, we'd better. Let them decide if they figure it could be connected to what's been happening."

"But I don't have to say that I saw my father's face."

When he hesitated, her heart began pounding in her ears. "If I did, they'd question him, wouldn't they?"

"I imagine so."

"And they'd tell him why. Cole, that would hurt him something awful, and that memory's wrong. Right this minute, he's downtown in his office. He wasn't the one shooting at us. And…oh, I'm only beginning to build a relationship with him again. I don't want it destroyed forever because of some memory I know can't be accurate."

She glanced uneasily over at her mother and Mark, then looked back at Cole. "You don't think Mark will decide this is a good chance to say something to the police, do you?"

"I don't know. Just let me think about the whole situation for a minute."

Looking away from Beth's anxious face, he tried to decide on the safest way to play things.

Glen Gregory's being in his office didn't mean as much as she apparently figured it did. He could have hired whoever was driving the Chevy—as well as whoever shot at them the other night, for that matter.

But given the way she was talking at the moment, if Niebuhr told the police she'd remembered her father as the murderer, she'd say he'd misunderstood her. And then…

Cole had already thought this through, so the pieces rapidly fell into place. Even if she admitted the truth, a recovered memory wouldn't give the police enough to charge Gregory. And while they were digging for more concrete evidence, he'd still be walking around free.

Since that was the case, what was the benefit to telling the police exactly what Beth had remembered?

There wasn't one, he decided. It would only upset her more. And if by any chance Gregory wasn't guilty, it would upset him, as well. Worse yet, if he *was* guilty, he'd probably feel pushed to make another attempt on her life—even sooner than he otherwise might have.

Cole looked at her again, trying not to think about anything terrible happening to her. But they could only be lucky so many times.

"Okay," he said. "Let's keep quiet about how specific your memory was. But you'd better take your uncle aside right now and remind him he promised you confidentiality."

IT WAS WELL PAST lunchtime before the detectives were done taking Beth's statement. When they escorted her back down the hallway to the front of the station, she saw that she'd been the last one to finish.

Mark and her mother were sitting on a bench, while Cole was talking with one of the detectives.

Her mother, she noted anxiously, looked extremely worried—which had to be because she knew that the shootings were probably related to her daughter's recovered memory.

The three of them spotted her at about the same moment, and her mother hurried over to hug her, Cole and Mark trailing behind.

"Oh, Beth," she said, holding her close. "I can't stop wishing you'd talked to me about this memory thing before you and Mark started in on it. It was just such a bad idea and—"

"It was not a bad idea," Mark interrupted.

Beth felt her mother tense.

"It's trying to keep traumatic memories repressed that's unhealthy," he went on. "And there was no conceivable way of knowing we'd end up with a mess like this.''

Her mother turned toward him, angrily saying, ''But we have, haven't we. And we have no idea who's trying to kill her—except that it's likely the same man who murdered Larisa. And do you think the police are going to figure out who he is this time around? Before he kills Beth?''

With that, her mother burst into tears.

''Aw, Mom,'' she murmured, hugging her again. ''I'm not going to get killed.''

''You almost did today.'' Her mother backed away a foot or so and made an effort to compose herself.

Finally, she looked at Mark. ''If only the police had found that journal. Even though it would have been too late for Larisa, at least we wouldn't be facing this now.''

''Journal?''

The way Cole said the word, Beth could tell he'd gone onto red alert.

''My sister kept a daily journal,'' her mother told him. ''But nobody could find the most recent one after she died. And we always thought that, if it had turned up, there might have been something in it that would have helped the police.''

''I never knew she kept a journal,'' Beth said.

''No, there was a lot you didn't know,'' her mother said slowly. ''And you were so close to Larisa that I always realized I should have talked to you about her as you got older. But each time I meant to, I ended up letting myself off the hook, rationalizing that it would be just too painful. Now, though, knowing you're in danger because of her…

''At any rate, she kept a journal from the time we were teenagers. Every night, before she went to bed, she'd write about her day. She had a pine blanket box, and after she finished writing she always locked the journal back into it. Journals, plural, as time passed, of course.

"When she died... She used to finish at least two or three of them a year, so that blanket box must have been almost full of them when she died. Was it, Mark?"

He silently nodded.

"Angela, let's get back to the missing one," Cole said.

"Well, she'd finished the latest one in the box a few months before she was murdered, and if only the police had found the current one... Well, as I said, it might have helped them, because there'd been a man visiting Larisa they couldn't identify, and—"

"They know all about that," Mark said. "I told you, they talked to the detective who was in charge of the case."

"But he didn't mention the journals," Cole said.

Mark shrugged. "They didn't learn anything useful from the ones that were there, so I guess he didn't think they were worth mentioning."

"But did they figure the killer might have taken the missing one?"

"I don't think so," Mark said slowly. "You see, Larisa was a real creature of habit. And she never had the journal out during the day, so it wouldn't have been just lying around for him to see.

"As Angela said, Larisa always took it out at night, then locked it back in the box after she finished writing. And the box was locked when she died. I mean, nobody had forced it open, looking for anything. But when the police opened it, there was no current journal inside."

"What about the earlier ones? Do you still have them?"

"No. I kept them for a while, but every time I looked at that box... I eventually got rid of them."

"You're sure there was one missing, though? That she was still keeping a journal when she died?"

"Frankly, I didn't know. I used to go to bed a little earlier than Larisa, and she'd do her writing after that. So she never mentioned that she'd stopped, but—"

"I'm positive she wouldn't have," Beth's mother said. "Not when she'd been keeping them for all those years."

After a moment's silence, she turned her attention back to Beth. "I want you to come and stay at the house with me."

"No, Mom, thanks for offering, but I'll be fine in my apartment."

"Fine? Darling, someone's trying to kill you."

"I think it would be a good idea," Mark said.

She looked at Cole, silently asking what he thought. She didn't like the idea of staying at her mother's, but she certainly didn't want to be on her own. And maybe he was getting tired of putting his life on hold to play bodyguard.

"Actually," he said, "I think Beth's better off at her own place."

Both her mother and Mark eyed him cooly, but he either didn't notice the sudden chill in the air or was choosing to ignore it.

"I've checked out her building and it's reasonably secure," he explained.

"But what about those phone calls?" Mark said. "They were making her nervous even before—"

"They're taken care of," Cole interrupted. "The

caller was a creep with a grudge, and the police charged him last night. At any rate,'' he added to Angela, ''Beth mentioned that your house is a big two story. I imagine there are a lot of potential ways into it?''

''I've never had a break-in.''

''Well, we wouldn't want to give someone a reason, would we.''

Beth felt icy fingers trailing up her back. Twice, the man with the gun had known exactly where and when to find her. And Cole was right. Breaking into her mother's house would be a piece of cake.

''What about coming and staying in my condo, then?'' Mark offered. ''We have tight security. And I don't like the thought of your being alone any more than your mother does.''

When she looked at Cole again, he raised his eyebrows a fraction of an inch. Obviously, if anybody was going to tell them, he wanted it to be her.

She cleared her throat. ''Actually, I haven't been alone. Since the first shooting, Cole's been sleeping on my couch.''

Her mother looked surprised.

Mark said, ''Oh?'' Then he focused on Cole. ''Didn't you think I'd like to know that? As a matter of fact, don't you think you should have told me about the first shooting? I asked you to keep me informed.''

''And I was doing that,'' Cole said evenly. ''But I didn't see any point in alarming you. Not when, for all we knew at the time, the shooting could have been meaningless—nothing more than some guy looking to take potshots at anyone he saw.''

''If you thought it was meaningless, why were you sleeping on her couch?''

"Mark?" Beth said. "You told him not to let anything happen to me. He was just doing his job."

When she looked at Cole again, the quirk of a smile he gave her said there was no way he'd just been doing his job. It made her heart skip a beat.

"And I'm glad he was," her mother said. "But you can't stay there indefinitely," she added to Cole.

"She won't need someone indefinitely," he said. "Only until we get to the bottom of things. Or, I should say, until the police get to the bottom of things. I've just been told to back off. They're treating the cemetery shooting as an attempted murder, and they don't want any civilian help with it."

"You're hardly a civilian," Beth said, trying to ignore the anxious feeling creeping through her. But if Cole was backing off...

Surely she hadn't misread that smile, had she? Surely he wasn't just going to desert her?

"Well, if you're not going to be involved any longer," her mother said to him, "Beth will have to come home with me."

"That gets us back to the problem of your house probably not being the safest place. But look, don't worry. I can arrange for someone to watch out for her."

"You mean a bodyguard?" Her mother turned to her. "Beth, if you need any money for that, just tell me."

Cole looked at her and smiled again—a warm, lazy smile this time.

She exhaled slowly. The message in his eyes was clear. He was going to keep on watching out for her.

And there was no one in the world she'd rather have as a bodyguard.

Chapter Twelve

Mark Niebuhr and Angela Gregory were already getting out of their cars when Cole pulled into her driveway.

"I'm sorry we had to come," Beth said for at least the third time.

He simply shrugged, although he was sorry, too. He wanted to get back to her apartment and figure out where they went from here.

The police might not want him having anything more to do with the case, but that was their problem. As long as someone was trying to kill her, nothing was going to stop him from trying to find out who it was.

"I'd have begged off," she said, "but they're upset enough as it is. If I'd broken with tradition..."

He reached over and squeezed her hand. "It's okay. I'm starving. So, as long as lunch is good, I'll be happy."

They climbed out of the Mustang and followed Niebuhr and Angela to the front door.

She slid her key into the lock, then murmured, "Oh, no."

"What's wrong?" Niebuhr demanded.

"It isn't locked," she said, her face pale. "And I know I locked it when I left."

"You're positive?" Beth asked.

"Oh, dear, you know that's one thing I never forget."

"Like Larisa," Niebuhr said quietly.

"She's right, she's very careful about the doors," Beth told Cole, looking frightened.

"You three stay here." He drew his gun. "I'll make sure there's nobody still inside."

"Shouldn't we call the police?" Niebuhr asked.

"Let me have a look first—in case she did just forget. There's no point wasting their time on a false alarm."

"Be careful," Beth whispered.

He opened the door and stepped into the foyer, then quietly reclosed it and stood listening. The house was silent.

Adrenaline pumping, he made himself wait for a full minute before starting cautiously forward.

Nothing seemed to be disturbed—unusual if there'd actually been a break-in. The living room looked as if a cleaning lady had just finished with it, and none of the drawers in the dining room were open.

He walked through to the kitchen, then into the family room beyond. There was a VCR on the shelf beneath the TV and a video camera sitting on an end table. Both were items that any self-respecting thief would have grabbed.

He'd almost decided that Angela *had* simply forgotten to lock up when he checked the sliding glass door leading out to the patio.

It, too, was unlocked, which blew that theory. Possibly, she'd missed locking one door. But if it was something she never forgot to do, she hadn't gone out and left two unlocked. Someone must have been in the house.

Retracing his steps along the center hall, he headed upstairs. The story was the same there. None of the rooms had been tossed, nothing was conspicuously out of place, and there were a couple of loose twenty-dollar bills sitting on the dresser in the master bedroom.

So what was the deal? It must have been someone who was only interested in something specific.

He headed back downstairs to have a look in the basement, although he doubted there'd be anything disturbed there, either. There were the standard furnace and laundry areas, plus a rec room with a couple of ground-level windows that looked out onto the driveway. Wandering over, he checked that both were locked, then slowly gazed around.

The dust on the furniture told him Angela didn't use the room much. But it looked as if she'd been down here sorting through her books. A couple of freestanding wooden bookcases—heavy ones that he'd guess were fifty or sixty years old—almost covered one wall. And several shelves of books had been taken down and were stacked on the floor.

She'd been doing the sorting recently, he decided on further inspection. There was no dust on the empty shelves.

After a final glance around, he headed back upstairs and along to the front door. When he opened it, the others eyed him expectantly.

"There's nobody inside," he told them. "And you were lucky," he added to Angela. "A lot of houses get trashed when there's a break-in, but there was nothing like that here. I have no idea what's missing, though. You'll have to figure it out.''

''We've already figured out how he got in,'' Beth said.

''Oh?''

''Remember the other night? How Mom's message said I should use the spare key if I wanted to stay here?''

''He found it?'' Cole said.

Angela nodded. ''I hide it under a rock in the garden and it's gone. We just checked.''

BETH DIDN'T THINK THAT either of the two uniformed officers who responded to their call looked old enough to be cops, but they arrived in a cruiser and she could see badges on their uniforms as they headed up the walk.

Cole opened the door to them, introducing her as Mrs. Gregory's daughter and himself simply as a friend of the family and the one who'd called to report the break-in. The officers proved to be constables Paul Gostick and Rosemary Westbury.

That established, Cole led the way down to the basement, where Beth's mother and Mark were waiting—under strict orders from Cole not to touch a thing.

After they got through the rest of the introductions, Paul took a notebook from his pocket and looked expectantly at Beth's mother.

She gestured toward the stacks of books. ''Those are the only things that seem to have been touched. I was down here yesterday, doing a load of wash, and they were on the shelves then. But when we came home today…"

The officers exchanged a glance; Beth could hardly blame them. What kind of nutcase broke into a house and did nothing but take a bunch of books off their shelves?

"So all that's missing are some books?" Paul said.

"Actually, as far as I can tell, there aren't any gone. Somebody just piled these ones on the floor."

"You mean *nothing* is missing? And nothing's been disturbed in the rest of the house?"

When her mother shook her head, Cole said, "She may notice, later, that things are missing."

"Yeah…of course," Paul said, not looking any less puzzled.

As he took a couple of steps forward, reaching toward one of the top books, Cole said, "Wait. Before you touch any of those, I should mention that the four of us were shot at this morning."

"Really?" Rosemary said. "You mean here, or…?"

"No, not here, and it's been reported. In fact, it was when we arrived here from Sixty-one Division that we discovered someone had been in the house. But under the circumstances, you might want to have somebody dust those books for prints."

Paul eyed Cole for a moment, as if tempted to ask who he thought he was, but finally just said, "He's right, Rosemary. Why don't you go put in a call for somebody."

"I was thinking there might have been some rare books among the others," Mark said as she headed for the stairs. "But Angela doesn't think there were."

She shook her head again. "If any of them were valuable, I never realized it. I don't think they'd have fetched more than a quarter each at a garage sale. And most of them have been sitting here for years. Beth and I bought those bookcases at an auction when she was only twelve or thirteen, and it didn't take long for them to fill up."

"And you've never hidden anything in the books?" Paul asked. "People sometimes hide money between the pages."

"I never have."

He glanced at Cole. "Could you tell how the intruder got in?"

"There was a front door key hidden in the garden. It's missing, and the door was unlocked when we got here."

Paul focused on Beth's mother once more. "And who knew where the key was hidden?"

"Nobody. I mean, nobody except my daughter. Oh, and I guess you knew, didn't you, Mark? I've used the same place forever, so Larisa probably mentioned it to you."

"If she did, I'd forgotten, but it wouldn't surprise me if she had."

"And you're certain there's nobody else?" Paul said to Angela.

"Yes. The next-door neighbors have a key, but I've never told them there was another one hidden."

"And you said you've been hiding it in the same place forever?" Cole asked.

"Uh-huh. Ever since we moved into the house, when Beth was just a toddler."

"Back when your ex-husband was living here."

Beth looked at Cole, wondering what on earth the

point of that remark was. Her father might have known where the key was hidden, but what would he want with some old books?

"Mrs. Gregory," Paul said, "I assume you won't be hiding a spare key in the future? And that you'll change the front door lock immediately?"

"Yes, Cole already called a locksmith for me."

"Good. Now, none of you saw any sign of the intruder when you arrived?"

"No. But I have a feeling he saw us," Cole offered.

"Oh?"

He gestured toward one of the windows. "That's Mrs. Gregory's car you can see in the driveway. So if someone was going through these books when she pulled in, he'd have spotted her."

"And taken off," Paul concluded.

Cole nodded. "Given the way the books are neatly stacked, I'd say he was intending to put them back on the shelves before he left—and probably put the key back, too. If he had, nobody would have realized he'd been here.

"But when we showed up, he left fast. There's a family room at the back of the main floor, and its door was unlocked, too. So while we were heading for the front door, he was probably going out the back."

"You should be a detective," Paul said.

"I am," Cole told him.

AFTER COLE PARKED in front of Beth's building, the way he carefully looked around made her nervous. But once they got out of the Mustang he took her hand, making her feel a lot better.

In fact, it seemed so right to be walking hand in hand with him that she couldn't help smiling. The way she'd come to feel about him made her certain she'd never really been in love with Brian. She'd never even been in the neighborhood.

"What are you smiling at?" Cole asked as they started up the front steps.

"Oh, just thinking about how your face dropped when my Mom finally served lunch."

He grinned. "You thought that was funny, eh? Well you've got a warped sense of humor, because I'm still starving."

"You could have eaten more."

"Beth, I don't consider a platter of raw fish edible."

"Not raw fish. Sushi."

"I know what it's called. But it still looks like something you should bait a hook with. And escargots?" he added as she unlocked the building's front door and they headed across to the elevator. "Real men don't eat snails, you know."

"Mark does. He loves them."

"Well he can have them. I mean, maybe I shouldn't be criticizing your mother's menu, but raw fish and snails and all those raw vegetables, and—"

"Crudités."

"What?"

"Served like that, they're called crudités."

"Yeah? I'd have thought they were called rabbit food."

"I told you she's a fitness nut. And she believes in healthy eating. But just to make it up to you, I've got a couple of steaks in the freezer. How does that sound for dinner?"

"I'd kill for a steak."

Beth winced. "Let's not talk about killing."

"Good idea."

The elevator's door opened and they stepped inside.

"Can we talk about fries, though?" he asked. "Fries with the steaks?"

"Absolutely. Unless I could interest you in a baked potato smothered in sour cream."

"Thank heavens you didn't inherit your mother's approach to eating." Cole gently brushed her hair back from her face while the door slid shut. A moment later he was kissing her—a long, deep kiss full of promise.

It made her knees weak and her insides melt. And made her suspect that, starving or not, he'd want to wait a while before they got around to dinner. Which was just fine with her.

"This elevator isn't slow enough," he murmured, releasing her when the door opened on the fourth floor.

"Rumor says it's the slowest elevator in the entire city," she teased.

He wrapped his arm around her waist and they walked down the hallway to her door.

As she unlocked it, he glanced at his watch. "It's only a couple of minutes until six. If there've been any developments about our shooting, they'll make the news."

They hurried through the office and into the living area. While Bogey and Bacall complained loudly about the lack of attention, Beth opened the armoire and switched on the television.

"Channel Nine okay?" Cole said, tossing his jacket and tie onto a chair and grabbing the remote.

That made her smile. Whenever she watched the news, she tuned in Channel Nine. And if their both liking the same news program—plus preferring steaks to sushi—wasn't an omen, she didn't know what was.

When he switched channels and got the start of a commercial, she said, "There must be time for me to feed the cats. If I don't, we'll hear more caterwauling than news."

Racing to the kitchen, she spooned out some food in record time and made it back to the living room before commercial number two was finished.

Cole patted the space on the couch beside him, then reached for her hand.

"I don't know why you'd want anything to do with a hand that looks like it's been holding a dozen leaky pens," she said, sinking down next to him.

The cops who'd come to dust the books had taken her prints, along with her mother's. Elimination prints, they'd called them. And fingerprint ink, she'd discovered, didn't just wash off with soap and water.

"You have the nicest ink-stained hands I've ever seen." He drew one to his lips and gave her fingers a sensuous nibble.

That made her insides melt again, but just as he wrapped his arm around her and pulled her close, the news logo appeared on the screen.

"Let's hold this thought for a minute," he said, lightly kissing her cheek, then focusing on the set.

A moment later the news anchor was saying, "In our top story of the day, Lesmill Cemetery was the scene of a drive-by shooting this morning. And our camera crew was there.''

Cole's arm tightened around her, and she wondered if he was feeling the same tension she was. Being with him made her feel so good that she kept almost forgetting someone was trying to kill her. But this was a definite reminder.

''He called it a drive-by,'' she pointed out. ''The police must not have said anything about treating it as attempted murder.''

''They always keep things from the media.''

On the screen, the anchor's face was replaced by announcer Karen Daily's. She was positioned at the side of the road, with Larisa's grave in the background of the camera's shot. The area directly surrounding it was roped off by yellow police tape.

''I'm standing in Toronto's Lesmill Cemetery,'' she began. ''Behind me is the grave of Larisa Niebuhr, a woman who, twenty-two years ago today, was brutally murdered in her home on Tranby Avenue.''

Karen paused while the camera zoomed in on the monument's inscription.

''This morning, tragedy nearly struck on the anniversary of her death. Four visitors to Mrs. Niebuhr's grave were almost gunned down in a drive-by shooting.

''The gunman was driving a late-model, dark blue Chevrolet. Anyone who saw a car matching that description in the vicinity of the cemetery at approximately ten o'clock this morning is asked to contact police at this number.''

A telephone number appeared in the top corner of

the screen, and the camera began to pan downward from the inscription.

"Fortunately," Karen continued, "the only damage done was to this marble dove that once graced the gravestone."

The camera came to rest on the dove, lying in the grass beside the monument.

"It fell to earth in a hail of bullets," Karen said softly.

"For Pete's sake," Cole muttered. "It's a lifeless hunk of stone."

"The police are refusing to release the names of those who were shot at," Karen continued. "But from other sources we've learned that each year three people visit the grave together on this day. They are the murdered woman's widower, her sister and a niece. After twenty-two years, these three still come to the graveside to pay their respects to Larisa Niebuhr."

The camera panned downward again, this time focusing in on the three bunches of roses.

"We should all hope to be so lovingly remembered," Karen said quietly. "Reporting from Lesmill Cemetery, I'm Karen Daily."

"In other news…" the anchor said, reappearing on the screen.

"Do you want to watch the rest of this?" Cole asked.

"Not unless you do."

He hit the remote, turning off the set, then pulled her close. She rested her head against his chest, breathing in his enticing scent.

"Beth," he whispered, "I'm not going to let anything happen to you, you know."

"I know," she whispered back. "You can leap tall buildings in a single bound. You've saved me from speeding bullets twice, so you're obviously faster than they are. And today my ankle didn't even get twisted in the process."

When he shifted so he could see her face, his smile sent her pulse racing.

"You have a warped sense of humor," he said.

His breath, warm against her cheek, almost made her forget about bullets and cemeteries and mysterious break-ins. When he was this near, it was hard to think about anything except him...and her...together.

Slowly, he trailed his knuckles down her cheek, then threaded his fingers through her hair. His touch made her want him to kiss her. And mind reader that he was, he did just that, cupping her chin in his hand and bringing his mouth to hers.

He kissed her softly at first, making her feel as if a warm, smoky haze was filling her body. Then the kiss grew deeper and more urgent, and her response was so strong it almost frightened her.

The smoky haze became a brush fire in her bloodstream, and she could feel his kiss everywhere. It made her breasts ache to be touched and her belly throb with desire.

Kissing him made her want so much more than mere kisses that when he eased her down onto the couch, stretching out so the lengths of their bodies were touching, a small, breathless whisper of desire rose in the back of her throat and escaped before she could even try to stop it.

"Beth," he murmured against her mouth. "I know

how fast this is, but I think I've fallen in love with you.''

It *was* fast. So fast that she wouldn't have believed him if she didn't think she'd fallen in love with him, too.

When she said that, he smiled the sexiest smile she'd ever seen, then slowly smoothed his hand down her back, drawing every inch of her tightly to him.

She could feel how hard his arousal was, and it made her wet with wanting. Sliding her hand down his body, she wordlessly told him so.

He groaned against her throat, started to kiss her again, then stopped and said, ''As much as I hate to even suggest moving, what are the odds a cat would land on us at a critical moment?''

That made her smile. And decide she liked a man who was wise to the ways of cats. ''The risk is probably pretty high,'' she told him.

Without another word, he rose and led her into the bedroom, firmly closing the door behind them, then leading her over to the bed.

''Now, where were we?'' he said.

''Cole, if you've forgotten, I'll never forgive you.''

''Well, don't worry, I think it's coming back to me.''

Slowly, his eyes not leaving hers, he reached around her and unzipped her dress, sliding both it and her slip off her shoulders.

When they dropped to the floor, he gazed at her for another moment, then quickly stripped naked.

She watched him, her eyes devouring him and her body aching for him.

He was all lean muscles, from his neck to his shoulders and down his chest, his skin bathed golden in the sunshine pouring through the skylight.

She let her eyes drift lower, liking everything she saw. And wanting it.

His clothes on the floor, he stepped back to where she was standing beside the bed and kissed her again, so hungrily that all she could think about was having him inside her.

Not breaking their kiss, he removed her bra and slid her panties down over her hips. Then he lowered her to the bed, pushing her panties the rest of the way off and covering her body with his.

She smoothed her hands down his back, pulling him closer, feeling his body heat mingling with hers, needing him to be part of her.

Greedily, he kissed her mouth, her throat, her breasts, until she could barely stand the exquisite torture any longer.

Finally, he slid his hand down between her legs, making her breath catch in her throat.

She was so warm and wet that when he entered her it was with one smooth thrust. She wrapped her legs tightly around him, and a moment later was moving with him, giving herself up to him, to the rhythm his body was setting and the smooth slide of his skin against hers.

With every thrust, she lost a little more of herself to his possession, until she felt that he was part of her and she was part of him.

Then heat began to drive away rational thought—heat from the sunshine, from Cole's body, from the blood pulsing through her veins.

Her breath began coming in short little gasps, until

she could scarcely breathe at all, and every nerve ending inside her body was crying out for more of him.

She didn't want the feeling to ever end. But if it didn't, she'd die. She'd shatter from the inside out.

Then Cole cried her name, thrusting even more deeply, and she did shatter, into a million tiny tremors that wouldn't stop sending delicious shivers through her body.

Cole lay on top of her, breathing hard, his sweat mingling with hers, until he finally eased onto his side and cuddled her to him.

Every time another of the little shivers seized her, she could feel him smiling against her neck.

"What are you thinking about?" he whispered at last.

Curling around in his arms, she tangled a little of his chest hair with her finger. "I'm thinking that for a woman who hasn't been very happy recently," she murmured, "I'm certainly making up for lost time."

Chapter Thirteen

The phrase ''died and gone to heaven'' had been drifting through Cole's mind during dinner.

Actually, it had begun its drifting long before that—back when he'd been kissing Beth on the couch. And then, once they'd moved to the bedroom...

Yes, this was definitely a ''died and gone to heaven'' type of situation he'd fallen into. And on top of everything else, she was a good cook.

''That was great,'' he told her, pouring the last of the burgundy.

''Better than sushi and escargots?''

''Marginally,'' he said, trying not to smile. He couldn't manage it, though. Every time he looked at her, he found himself smiling.

Of course, if he really didn't want to, he simply had to remember that someone was trying to kill her.

''Want to move into the living room?'' she suggested.

''Sure.'' He picked up his wineglass and followed her to the couch.

''You know what I've been thinking about?'' he

said, sinking down beside her and draping his arm cozily over her shoulders.

"Me?"

"Well, yeah. Mostly about you. But a little bit about that missing journal of Larisa's. Assuming she was still keeping one when she died, why wasn't it in the blanket box?"

"I don't know."

"Dammit," he muttered. "I wish we knew how to get hold of Abbot in Calgary. I'd like to ask him what conclusion they came to about it. But if there *was* a current diary, and the killer didn't take it, then Larisa must have had it hidden away—someplace other than in the blanket box, and well enough that the police couldn't find it."

"Why would she have hidden it?"

"Who knows? But if she did, there's a chance it's still wherever she stashed it."

"You mean still in the house? After all these years?"

"It must be, unless somebody found it and threw it out. And if it *is* there, I'd sure like to have a look at it."

Beth's pulse skipped a beat. "The mystery man? You think his name might be in it?"

"Well...there might be something. Some clue, although I doubt we'd get his name. I can't imagine Larisa would have written about her affairs. She'd have known there was always a chance Mark would see those journals."

"But even a clue..." Thinking that would be more than they had at the moment, Beth closed her eyes.

"What?" Cole said after a moment. "You think better with your eyes shut?"

"Not think, but remember," she explained. "It's a trick Mark taught me. When he was trying to help me remember, he was always telling me to close my eyes and let my memory paint a picture—so let me get back to it."

"In other words, keep quiet."

She smiled without opening her eyes. "In other words, yes."

Trying to force away all thoughts of the present, she created a mental picture of the living room in the house on Tranby Avenue.

The image formed clearly in her mind's eye, but no memories came to her. Next, she pictured the dining room. Then the kitchen.

After that produced nothing, she went through the same process with the rooms on the second floor—with no more positive results than she'd had with the main floor. That left only the attic.

She didn't want to imagine it. She'd seen it too many times in her nightmares to want to dredge up a picture of it. But, her heart beating faster, she forced herself to do exactly that—imagining it was the day of the murder, picturing herself heading up into the attic after Larisa.

They were going to play dress-up, so she happily followed her aunt up the steep stairs, barely noticing the way the dust began to tickle her nose as they reached the top.

"Now, let's see," Aunt Larisa said, stopping and looking around. "I think there's some really good stuff in this trunk. Just give me a minute to get it out."

While Aunt Larisa opened the trunk, Beth started across to the window. If there were people in the street, when she looked down it was like she was a big giant and they were little—

"Oops!" she said, almost falling.

"What's wrong?" Aunt Larisa asked.

"There's a loose board. I tripped."

She reached down to push it flat, but before she could touch it, Aunt Larisa said, "Oh, just wait a second, Beth. I'll fix it."

A moment later, Aunt Larisa was kneeling beside the board and pushing it into place.

"It needs new nails," Beth said.

"Oh...well..." Aunt Larisa wiped her forehead with her hand, then gave Beth a funny-looking smile. "It's never been sticking up like that before, so it'll be okay."

"But it might not be. I could ask Uncle Mark to nail it for you."

"Aah...no. That wouldn't be a good idea."

"He wouldn't mind."

Aunt Larisa reached for Beth's hands. "I'm going to tell you a secret, all right?"

Beth grinned. She loved secrets.

"But you have to promise not to tell *anyone*. Not even your mom or dad. And not Uncle Mark."

"Okay."

"Well...I don't want the board nailed, because I have to be able to move it up and down."

"Why?"

Aunt Larisa didn't answer for a minute, but finally said, "Now remember, this is a *serious* secret."

"I'll remember."

"All right, then. You see, underneath the board is my secret hidey-hole."

Beth exhaled slowly, her heart suddenly pounding.

"I might know," she whispered, opening her eyes. "Cole, I might know where the journal is."

Quickly, she filled him in.

"Then the only question," he said when she was done, "is how do we get into that attic?"

"Wait a minute," she said slowly. "Couldn't you get in trouble if you went looking for evidence after the police told you to butt out?"

"A journal wouldn't technically be evidence. Legally, it would be considered hearsay. And if it contained any clues, I'd let the police know. But look, let's not worry about the fine points right now. We might not even get into the house. And if we do, there might not be any journal."

"But if there is?"

"Then I'll figure out the best way to handle things."

"And you're sure there'd be no trouble."

"None I couldn't take care of. So don't worry, okay?"

She eyed him for a moment, thinking of something he'd said the first day in his office—that he knew how far he could go without endangering his license. So, if he was saying he could take care of things, she'd just have to believe him.

"All right," she said at last. "Why don't we simply phone whoever owns the house now? And explain that we think there might be something in the attic, and... But I guess the explaining part could get tricky, couldn't it."

Cole nodded. "They'd ask a lot of questions. Like what do we think's up there and why do we want it? And what do you figure they'd do the minute they hung up the phone?"

"Aah, I see what you're getting at. They'd search the attic."

"Exactly. And if they found the journal and realized it was Larisa's, they—"

"But how would they?"

"Because they've got to know about the murder. If they didn't before they bought the house, some of the neighbors would have given them all the gory details after they moved in.

"And I assume that even if Larisa's name isn't on the journal, she dated her entries. So, if they realized this was a journal that was being kept in the months before the murder, they might decide to give it to the police rather than us. And we've got a whole lot more incentive to get to the bottom of things fast than the police do."

An only-too-familiar feeling of unease began curling around in Beth's mind. Their "whole lot of incentive" was that if they didn't identify the murderer fast enough, he'd have another try at killing her.

"But just showing up at the door isn't a good idea, either," Cole was saying. "Not many people would let a couple of total strangers go poking around in their attic."

"Not even when one of them's a private investigator?"

He shook his head. "No, we need some sort of edge, something that'll get us in without having to give up the element of surprise. But what?"

Beth tried to think. "How about Esther Voise?" she said at last. "Would she help us?"

Cole grinned. "You know, I think she might. She struck me as a woman who'd love a little intrigue in her life."

Five minutes later, Beth was anxiously watching him pace the room, the cordless in his hand.

"Well, thanks again, Miss Voise," he said. "I can't tell you how much we appreciate this."

"All set," he said, clicking off. "We make her place our first stop, then she takes us across the street and introduces us to the current lady of the house— a Marilyn Williamson."

"Esther figures she'll be there?"

"Uh-huh. She's some sort of freelancer who works at home."

THE NEXT MORNING, as Esther Voise was ringing the bell of the Tranby Avenue house, Cole leaned closer to Beth and whispered, "You going to be okay?"

"I don't know," she said honestly.

She'd woken in the middle of the night with another of her attic nightmares. But at least, this time, Cole had been right there beside her to wrap his arms around her, hold her until her fear subsided, and then make love with her.

It had made all the difference in the world, and having him with her now was making her far less anxious than she'd otherwise be. Still, despite the warmth of the July morning, the prospect of going up into that attic was giving her goose bumps.

Esther was just reaching out to ring again when a middle-aged woman opened the door.

"Good morning," Esther greeted her. "I'm sorry if I'm disturbing your work, but I've brought over a couple of people who'd like to talk to you for a minute."

"Oh?" The woman looked curiously at Beth and Cole.

"They're private investigators—Cole Radford and Wendy Kinahan. This is Marilyn Williamson," she added, glancing at Cole and Beth.

Beth forced a smile, feeling guilty about carrying on their Wendy Kinahan subterfuge when Esther was being so helpful. But if they'd come clean and admitted they'd initially lied to her, she might not be so helpful.

"They talked to me about a few things the other day," Esther continued. "And now something's come up about your house."

"*My* house?"

"Yes, you see, they're working for Dr. Niebuhr. The man who owned it way back. You know, the one who's wife…"

Marilyn nodded. "Well…come in."

"Thank you," Cole said. "We'll take as little time as possible, but we think there may be a diary of Mrs. Niebuhr's in your attic. And if there is, we wondered… It would mean a lot to Dr. Niebuhr if he could have it."

Beth held her breath. The request sounded perfectly innocent to her. But did it to Marilyn Williamson?

"I've never noticed a diary up there," she said. "And the house had other owners after Dr. Niebuhr—before my husband and me, I mean. If there ever was a diary, it's probably long gone."

"Not necessarily," Cole said. "It was hidden away, but we know where. So if you could see your way clear to just let us have a quick look…"

When Marilyn didn't reply immediately, Esther said, "Dr. Niebuhr's a very nice man. And if it would mean a lot to him…"

Marilyn shrugged. "I guess it couldn't hurt to let you look."

Beth exhaled slowly, silently thanking Esther as the four of them started for the second floor.

With each stair they climbed, she could feel her anxiety level rising. When they got to the upstairs hallway, she reached for Cole's hand, afraid that being in the hall would trigger an image of the murder.

But with different wallpaper and carpeting, it no longer looked the way it had, and it wasn't until Marilyn opened the door to the attic that Beth's heart began to hammer.

The narrow stairway looked exactly the same, right down to the dust motes lazily floating in the hot air.

It smelled the same as well. Dry and stale, like the air in a cottage when it's first opened after a long, unoccupied winter.

"I'm not sure I can do this," she whispered to Cole.

"I can go up and look on my own," he whispered back. "I know roughly where it is."

As tempting as the offer was, she shook her head. Surely, in the long run, confronting her demons would be better than running away from them. "I'll give it a try," she murmured.

Her heart pounding harder still, she followed Marilyn up the steep stairs. Even with Cole's hand resting reassuringly against the small of her back, she felt physically ill by the time they reached the attic.

Forcing herself to start walking forward, she kept her gaze on the floor until she spotted the board. Then she stood staring at it, unable to make herself bend down.

But, after a moment, Cole was kneeling beside her, saying, "This looks like what we were told about, right? Just let me work it out."

He applied pressure to first one end of the board and then the other, gradually wiggling it up. When he finally pulled it free, Beth's breath caught in her throat. There was a faded red notebook in the space.

He took it out and glanced through the first few pages, looking so unimpressed that her hopes sank. Maybe it wasn't the missing journal at all. Maybe Larisa had hidden something else here.

But then he said, "I think this is what we're looking for," and her hopes began climbing toward the sky. If it was the mystery man who was trying to kill her, and the journal helped them learn who he was...

"This is going to make Dr. Niebuhr awfully happy," Cole said. Then he glanced at Marilyn. "Oh, I'm sorry. I shouldn't just *assume* that you won't mind us taking it for him."

"Well...I guess...if it was his wife's."

Cole pushed himself up and crossed the attic to where Marilyn and Esther Voise were standing. "Here's her name on the cover," he said, showing it to them. "See. Larisa Stinson Niebuhr, Journal number fifty-two."

THE MINUTE THEY PULLED away from the curb, Beth opened the journal to the first page and began skimming the entries.

"Anything?" Cole said, glancing over as he turned onto Avenue Road.

"Not so far. There's no mention of any men except Mark."

She went back to her skimming, a sinking feeling

in the pit of her stomach. What if Larisa had censored her writing so completely that there wasn't even a clue?

Turning another page, she started in on the next entry. "Oh, my Lord," she murmured, reading it.

"What?" Cole demanded.

"It's here," she whispered, her mouth so dry she could barely speak. "Listen to this—the entry dated July 1.

"'Today, I made a decision that will turn my life upside down. I'm going to leave Mark for Dennis Roth. I know people will think I'm crazy to leave a psychiatrist for a starving artist—with a ponytail no less—but that's what I'm going to do.'

"Ponytail," she repeated for emphasis. "Cole, that has to be the mystery man!"

He reached over and gave her hand a squeeze. "Hallelujah. I didn't think we'd actually get his name."

"Well, we did. So now what do we do?"

"We go back to your place and check the phone book. And if there's no listing for him, we turn on the computer and start checking databases. Between city directories, public records, credit records and whatever, it's not usually too tough to track people down.

"But what else does it say?" he asked, gesturing toward the journal.

Her heart beating rapidly, Beth turned her attention back to the entry she'd been reading.

"'In all the time Mark and I have been married,'" she continued, "'I've never written down a word about any of my affairs—since that's all they were. Transient affairs I needed because my sex drive is so strong while Mark's is virtually nonexistent. The other men never meant anything to me, but it's entirely different with Dennis.

"'I can't begin to describe how I feel when I'm with him, but I can barely believe how much I love him. Or how much he loves me. I dream of him all night and think about him every minute I'm awake. I can't live without him. And I can't live with Mark when I'm in love with another man.

"'So I've made my decision, for better or worse— although I've thought of a way to ensure it will undoubtedly be for the better. The only things left to decide are exactly when I'll leave and how I'll tell Mark.

"'That's a moment I'm already dreading. Perhaps it would be best to simply leave him a note when I go. That would be the coward's way, of course, but I've never been a very brave person.'"

Beth flipped to the following page and let her eyes fly over it. "The next entries talk about Dennis, too," she told Cole. "More of the same. About his visits, and how desperately she loves him, and agonizing about telling Mark."

"Keep going. See if you find anything different. Maybe she'll talk about a fight or something. If it was Dennis who killed her, he had to have a reason."

Rapidly, Beth worked her way through more entries. "Here's something different," she said at last. "But it's not about him.

"'July 22,'" she read. "'I had the scare of my life today. I wasn't feeling well, so I slept in and let Mark make his own breakfast. And when I finally went down to the kitchen, I discovered that I'd forgotten to lock my journal away last night.

"'After I wrote in it, I put it on the counter while I made some tea. Then I just left it there and went to bed.

"'I've never been that careless before, and it makes me wonder if, subconsciously, I *wanted* Mark to read it.

"'I don't know. But consciously, that's that last thing I'd want. So thank heavens he didn't. I'm positive he couldn't have, or he'd have come roaring upstairs like a charging rhino.

"'But what if I hadn't been lucky and he *had* read it? Or what if he starts to suspect something? I'm sure I can't be acting normally these days, so what if he notices and decides that reading my journal might be a good idea?

"'I'm probably being paranoid, but what if I'm not? If he wanted to, I know he could get my blanket box open. So I think I'd better start keeping this journal in a different place, just in case.

"'From now on, I'll be making a little trip into the attic after I finish my daily writing. The journal will be safe up there, and the exercise can only do me good.'"

"And that was dated?" Cole said.

"July 22."

"Five days before the murder. Read through the rest of the entries. See if she says Mark's acting strange or anything. If she decides that maybe he did read the journal."

Her pulse racing, Beth read the remaining entries. The final one was dated July 26.

"Nothing," she said, finishing it. "Just more agonizing about exactly when she was going to leave. But... You think maybe Mark *knew?*"

"He obviously could have."

"But…" A horrifying thought popped into Beth's mind. A second later, she realized it wasn't even a possibility.

"Mark was in his office when Larisa was murdered," she said. "Abbot told us his secretary confirmed that, remember?"

"I remember. But if Mark *did* know…"

"What?" she demanded.

Cole shrugged. "Abbot told us a lot of things. Including that the murderer could have been a hired hit man."

THERE WERE STILL a dozen questions rattling around in Cole's brain when he and Beth arrived back at her apartment.

Had Niebuhr read Larisa's journal? he asked himself while she unlocked the door. Learned about her affair with Dennis Roth? he added, stepping into Beth's office.

"We need to put the journal someplace safe," he told Beth.

"We're not giving it to the police?"

"Uh-huh, but not just yet."

"That couldn't be a problem for you?"

"No, I told you, a journal would only be considered hearsay, so it's not like withholding evidence."

"But it suggests that Mark had a motive."

"Right, but we wouldn't know there's anything of interest to the police until we'd read it, and who's to know we've done that yet?"

"I could lock it in my desk. It would be safe there."

As she opened the desk, Cole absently leaned

down to stroke Bogey and Bacall, who'd come to the door to greet them, and went back to thinking about those questions that were nagging at him.

If Niebuhr had found out about Dennis Roth, what were the odds that Glen Gregory wasn't guilty? And that Roth wasn't, either? Could the good doctor have actually been behind Larisa's death?

He followed Beth into the apartment, telling himself that if they could locate Roth and get his story, they might have a better idea of what was what.

"Someone called," he said, noticing the message light blinking on Beth's machine.

After she pushed Play, there was a moment of silence. Then a worried voice Cole wouldn't have recognized said, "Beth, it's your father. I...I'm sorry. This is a terrible message to leave on a machine, but I want you to hear it from me, and for the life of me I can't remember your cell phone number."

She glanced anxiously at Cole, then turned her attention back to the machine. He wrapped his arm around her shoulders as the message continued.

"Beth...I've been arrested. Charged with murdering Larisa. I didn't do it. I hope that goes without saying. But the police said they found some evidence and..."

They'd found *evidence?* Cole could hardly believe it. Just when he'd started thinking that Gregory might not be guilty as sin, the cops had found enough evidence to charge him.

"I don't think I'm making much sense here," he was saying. "But...look, maybe you'd better call your mother. They said the evidence was in the house and... She must know more of the details than I do. I'll call you again after I've seen my lawyer. He said he'd be here as soon as he could and... Well, they told me I'm allowed reasonable use of a phone, so I'll call you again."

There was a click, then silence.

"Oh, Lord," Beth murmured. "I've got to go and see him. But where is he?"

"It doesn't much matter. Seeing him won't be an option."

"What?"

"Beth, he's been charged with murder. Only his lawyer will get to see him without facing a ton of red tape."

"Then what do I do? How am I going to find out what's going on? Does he know I remembered him as the killer?"

"No," she said, shaking her head and answering her own question. "The way he was talking, he can't know. But did Mark tell the police, and is that why they arrested him?"

Cole thought about that for a couple of seconds, then said, "If Mark had told them, they'd already be considering you a witness, so they wouldn't have let your father call you."

"A witness? *Against* him?"

"Hey, take it easy," he said, drawing her close. "We don't really know what's happening yet."

"But he said evidence. What *kind* of evidence? And what house was he talking about? The one on Tranby? It almost sounded as if he meant my mother's."

Not knowing the answers any more than she did, Cole simply held her, resting his chin on her head and breathing in the fresh scent of her hair. When she made a sad little noise against his shoulder, he began wishing he could magically do away with all the evils in her life.

Unfortunately, he was no magician. He was just an ordinary man who had to work through things one step at a time. And in this case, if Gregory figured his ex-wife would know the details, step one was having Beth phone her mother and find out what the hell they were.

When she called, the line was busy. She fed the cats, looking as if she was about to start crying any second, then tried the number again.

"It's still busy," she said, putting down the phone. "She probably has it off the hook."

"Does she do that?"

"Yes, whenever something stresses her out and she doesn't want to talk to anyone."

"Well, let's not worry about what *she* wants just now. Let's go pay her a visit."

Chapter Fourteen

The Taurus was in the driveway, but nobody responded to Beth's knock. She was certain her mother was home, though. Not answering the door was another of her coping mechanisms.

"Mom," she called loudly, knocking again. "Mom, it's me, open up."

"Try to relax," Cole said. "We'll learn exactly what's happened, then we'll figure out what to do."

His words made her feel a tiny bit better. Even though her world was swinging wildly out of control, he was such an anchor of sanity that, once again, she just didn't know what she'd do without him.

When her mother finally opened the door, she looked as if she'd been crying for a week. She also looked as if she'd taken some of the anxiety pills that her doctor prescribed and Beth worried about.

"Oh, Beth," she sobbed, falling into her arms.

Beth took a slow, deep breath. She felt like crying, too. She'd been fighting back tears ever since she'd listened to her father's message. But letting herself disintegrate wouldn't help matters.

"Let's go sit down," she said, guiding her mother

toward the living room. "We need you to fill us in on things."

By the time they were seated on the couch and Cole had pulled a chair over so he could sit facing them, her mother had managed to stop crying and was beginning to ask questions.

"Beth, why didn't you tell me exactly what you'd remembered? And why wouldn't you go to the police? Mark said you insisted on saying nothing, but if your father..." She paused to wipe away fresh tears. "How could you have known he did it and think he shouldn't have to pay?"

"Mom, I never *knew* he did it. And neither did Mark. He just—"

"Beth, he told me everything. And he told the police, as well."

"Oh, no. You don't mean he told them I remembered Dad as the murderer."

When her mother nodded, she looked at Cole, her stomach in so many knots it felt like a solid lump. "You said Mark couldn't have told them. That if he had, they wouldn't have let my dad call me."

"They shouldn't have. Whoever did must have been missing a few facts."

"But if they have rules like that... He won't be able to call me again, will he? And I won't ever be able to see him, will I?"

"Darling, why would you want to?" her mother said.

"Because he's my father!"

"Beth...he's a murderer. He murdered Larisa."

"No," she whispered. "How can you say anything that horrible?"

"Darling...I'm going to tell you something I

swore I never would. When you were just a little girl, your father and Larisa had an affair.''

"No," she whispered again, feeling as if someone were tearing her insides out.

"Yes. It was a couple of years before her death. And when I found out about it... Well, I talked to Mark, and we confronted the two of them. And they both swore it was already over and they knew it had been a terrible mistake and...

"At any rate, I tried to forgive them. I did my best, Beth. I acted as if Larisa and I were still close and I tried to keep loving your father. But he'd screwed around with my *sister!*

"I guess Mark handled things better than I did. He was able to forgive Larisa. Of course, as far as he knew—until after her death, at least—she'd only had the one affair.''

Unless, Cole thought, he had read that journal.

"But I could never really forgive either one of them," Angela continued.

Cole eyed her as she spoke, wondering again about *her* being the murderer. After all, given what he'd heard about Larisa, she'd probably instigated the affair. And maybe Angela's resentment had festered and grown until it was too much to bear.

That thought lingering in his mind, he glanced at Beth and realized she was looking more distraught than he'd ever seen her. He covered her hand with his, wishing he could get her out of here right now. But they couldn't leave until they knew what the entire story was.

"Angela?" he said. "It would really help if you walked us through what's happened in the past little while. Exactly what happened that led to Mr. Gregory's arrest?''

''I don't know where to start.''

''How about starting back at yesterday afternoon. What happened after Beth and I left?''

''Nothing,'' Angela said, clearly trying to control her emotions. ''Not right away. Mark stayed for another cup of coffee, then he left, too. But he called later, after dinner, and said he'd been thinking about those books and was coming back over.

''And when he got here, he said that he was wondering if we'd been on the wrong track. If maybe the intruder hadn't really been interested in the books, but had only been taking them down so he could move the bookcases and get at something behind them.''

''What would have made him think that?''

''That's exactly what I asked him. And it was then he told me he thought it was Beth's father who'd been in here. And that he might have hidden something behind a wall panel—years ago, long before I had those bookcases.''

Angela began playing with a loose strand of her hair, looking incredibly anxious. ''That he might have hidden something to do with the murder,'' she finally added. ''Because Beth had remembered seeing Glen kill Larisa. I almost couldn't believe it when he told me that.

''But *he* believed it. He said that maybe they'd started up together again and then had a fight and... Oh, he was only guessing about the details, but he wanted to have a look behind the paneling. So we moved everything, and he pried a couple of the panels loose and...there it was. Stashed behind one of them.''

"There what was?" Cole said, his adrenaline pumping.

"The evidence," she murmured. "The knife Glen used to murder Larisa."

Cole's heart thudded against his ribs. "You mean you assumed that's what it was."

"What else could it have been? It was wrapped in a piece of bloodstained white terry cloth, inside a freezer bag. But the handle wasn't covered, so we could see it was a knife. And when the police came and we told them everything, *they* certainly assumed it was that knife.

"It was...one from my own kitchen. A special one that had been a gift, and I recognized it—even though it had gone missing decades ago. After that we told the police that Beth had remembered her father as the murderer. And that Glen and Larisa had once been lovers. And when Mark said he thought they might have started up again, and... Well, with the murder weapon having come from my kitchen, and it being hidden right here in what had been Glen's house, they obviously decided they had enough to arrest him.''

WHILE COLE CLOSED the passenger's door and walked around to the driver's side, Beth did her best to keep holding back her tears. But she'd reached the breaking point, and by the time he opened his own door she was crying.

"Hey." He slid into the car and wrapped his arms around her. "Things aren't always as bad as they seem."

"But this time they are," she managed to say. "Oh, Cole, he had an affair with his own sister-in-law. And then he killed her. It was him all along."

"I'm not so sure."

"What?" When she sat back and looked at him, he shook his head.

"I know I only met your father once, but he struck me as both intelligent and logical."

"He is," she said, wiping her eyes. "So how could he have even gotten involved with Larisa in the first place?" How could her own father...? She could hardly bear to think about it.

"Things like that happen," Cole said gently. "You know they do. Nobody's perfect. And from the sounds of things, if Larisa decided she wanted a man, she had what it took to get him."

Cole started the engine and backed out of the driveway before he went on. "But having an affair is one thing, and committing murder's something else," he said as they started down the street. "And if your father killed her, why on earth would he have kept the knife? And hidden it in his own house, of all places? Wrapped in what must have been a piece of the bathrobe? Why wouldn't he have taken the robe and that sports bag Abbot mentioned out into the country and burned them? Why wouldn't he have wiped the knife clean and dropped it into the middle of Lake Ontario?"

Beth couldn't come up with a logical answer to any of those questions, but since she didn't think very well when she was upset, she was afraid to let her hopes rise.

When Cole didn't continue, though, she said, "You're really thinking he didn't kill Larisa, then?"

"I was having an easier time believing he did before there was this evidence. He's just too smart to have stashed incriminating evidence in his own house."

Beth gazed at Cole, reminding herself he was a trained detective. So maybe things weren't as bad as they seemed—although she had trouble believing that was possible.

"Then how are you putting the pieces together now?" she asked.

"I'm not entirely sure. But, first off, we can rule out Dennis Roth. There's no way he'd have broken into your parents' house to steal that knife, murdered Larisa, then broken in again to stash it in the wall. Even if he knew where they lived, why would he risk getting caught breaking in? Twice, yet. No, if *he'd* killed Larisa, the murder weapon wouldn't have come from your parents' kitchen."

"But if he didn't do it, why didn't he come forward and talk to the police?"

"And tell them what? That he and Larisa had been having an affair? Beth, he probably figured nobody else knew about them. And I'm just guessing here, but I'll bet that if he had no idea who killed her, if he figured nothing he could tell the cops would be any help, he decided he'd be smarter to keep his mouth shut. After all, it would have occurred to him that they'd suspect *he* might have murdered her. So, especially if he didn't have an alibi for the morning she was killed…

"Well, we may never know the actual story as far as he's concerned, but let's get back to that damn knife in the wall. I'd say the only people who might conceivably have put it there were your father, your mother or Mark.''

"My mother or Mark? But if you don't think it was my father... You're saying that one of *them...?*''

"Let's start with Mark.''

Start with him? And then go on to the possibility that her *mother...?* No, that just wasn't a possibility.

Not that she could believe her uncle was, either, but she forced her thoughts to him. Had Cole progressed from wondering if Mark might have read Larisa's journal and hired a hit man to deciding that's what had actually happened? Was he saying that if her father wasn't guilty, then her uncle had to have been behind things? Or, worse yet, her mother?

"Mark always knew where the spare key was hidden," he was saying. "Your mother mentioned something about that yesterday. Which means he could easily have gotten in to steal the knife, and then again to hide it. So let's consider what's been happening lately, and figure out if there's any of it that Mark *couldn't* have been involved with.

"He certainly could have hired that guy in the coveralls and gorilla mask. And the one taking potshots at us in the cemetery. And that car following us the other day, the one we assumed was your father's, didn't have to be. I mean, you were right. There might not be many cars like his in Toronto, but there has to be more than one. Maybe Mark got it from some luxury car rental place.

"And I told him that we were going to see Mrs. Voise. So if he *had* rented a look-alike car, and wanted us to figure your father was spying on us..

"And he could have easily paid someone to go into your mother's house yesterday, and take those books off the shelf—probably hoping that, when she called the cops, they'd think of the possibility that something was hidden behind the bookcase. Then, when they didn't, he raised it himself.''

Beth anxiously waited for Cole to voice a conclusion about all those ''could haves.'' When he didn't, she finally said, ''Then there's nothing that rules Mark out?''

''Not that I can see. But not ruling him out isn't the same as proving he's been orchestrating things— or that he was behind Larisa's murder. Which means we should go back to that and think motive. If he *did* read the journal, if he knew Larisa was planning to leave him for Roth…''

Cole was silent for a minute, then looked across the car. ''Isn't there something called false memory syndrome? Isn't that part of the whole debate about recovered memories? Aren't some experts very dubious about their accuracy?''

''I…'' Her thoughts began to race. ''From what I've read,'' she said at last, ''I gather a lot of experts are convinced that if a therapist raises a possibility enough times during sessions—subtly, I mean, without the patient even realizing what's going on… Well, yes, then the patient comes to believe something happened that didn't.''

''Or comes to believe she saw something differently than she really did?'' Cole said. ''When Mark was supposedly trying to help you remember what you saw, couldn't he have done something to make you *think* it was your father who killed Larisa?''

''I imagine it's possible,'' she murmured. But would Mark really have ''helped'' her remember seeing her father? She could hardly believe he might have, yet he definitely *had* talked about her father during their sessions. And if he'd implanted the image she'd eventually ''remembered''...

If he had, would that explain why she'd doubted, all along, that her memory was accurate? Explain why, in the back of her mind, she'd been convinced that something *had* to be wrong with it?

Her hands had begun to tremble so she clasped them together. The thought that Mark might have intentionally messed with her mind was making her positively ill.

''So,'' Cole said slowly, ''if he wanted to keep you from remembering the real killer... But, dammit, why would he care? I mean, even if he's guilty, even if the killer was someone he hired, what could you have given the police to go on? The description of a stranger you saw, under traumatic circumstances, twenty-two years ago? When you were eight years old?

''Hell, he'd be insane if he was worried about that. He'd only have had reason to worry if he'd committed the murder himself.''

''And we know he didn't. He was in his office all that morning.''

''Yeah...unless his secretary lied.''

That started more than just Beth's hands trembling. If Mark had killed Larisa, and if he'd been afraid she'd remember that... If his choice had been between letting her remember what she'd actually seen or making her remember the killer as someone else...someone like her father, whom he might have secretly hated because of her father's affair with Larisa...

''Let's run with the possibility that Mark read Larisa's journal and then murdered her himself,'' Cole said. "By the time he killed her, she was hiding the journal in the attic. So even though he'd have wanted to destroy it, he couldn't find it. But he knew the police might. And if they got their hands on it, they'd have learned she was intending to leave him for Dennis Roth. And they'd have assumed Mark might have known, which would have given him a motive for murder. So, while your father would have been crazy to hide the murder weapon if *he'd* killed Larisa, it would have been a smart move for Mark.''

Beth shook her head. "You've lost me.''

"Well, once he'd planted the evidence, if the police had come to suspect him, he could somehow have made sure they found out where the knife was—which would have incriminated your father. And hell, that explains something else, too.''

"What?'' she said.

"A hit man's first priority would have been destroying the evidence. So if Mark was using a hit man, how did he get the knife and that piece of bathrobe? Can you imagine a professional killer handing over anything that could incriminate him?''

She shook her head, although imagining hit men's behavior was hardly her specialty.

"At any rate, as things turned out, the police bought Mark's alibi. So he had no reason to worry about whether they found the knife or not. Not until that memory of yours started to surface.

"But once it did, he knew that sooner or later you'd probably recall everything—including the fact that *he* murdered Larisa.''

"Then why did he help me remember in the first place?''

"Because he figured you'd eventually remember with or without his help. And the way he handled things, he was able to make you remember your father instead of him."

"Cole...you sound so certain he's guilty."

"I'm not. Not entirely. But things sure add up nicely, don't they?" He paused, shaking his head, then said, "You know, if it *was* him, he's played things perfectly. Now that the police know you remembered the killer as your father, even if your memory does get more accurate, Mark won't have a thing to worry about. If you change your story, the cops will figure you're only trying to save your father."

"But...that just shouldn't be!" She swallowed hard, suddenly close to tears once more.

"I know. But if Mark is guilty, and we can figure out how to prove it..."

When Cole flicked on the turn signal, she glanced out of the car window and saw that they'd reached Wilson Place.

He made the turn, then said, "Dammit."

She looked out of the Mustang and saw a nondescript dark car parked outside her building.

"Police detectives," Cole told her.

"Oh, Lord. Do I have to admit that Mark was telling the truth? That I remembered my father as the killer?"

"'Fraid so."

"But you'll be right there with me?"

"They'd never let me sit in."

Her stomach lurched. She didn't feel in any shape to face a couple of cops on her own.

"You're entitled to have a lawyer present," Cole

said. "And I do a lot of work for lawyers. If you want, we can get the best one who can free up some time."

"Then let's."

She'd barely uttered the words before she wondered if she was overreacting. After all, *she* wasn't at risk of being charged with anything.

A lawyer wouldn't let her say something she shouldn't, which was the last thing she wanted to do. If she had to tell the truth, she would, but the less she said that would harm her father, the better. Because at this point, she was absolutely certain she'd remembered the wrong face.

Cole pulled the Mustang to a stop behind the parked car, then reached into the glove compartment for his cellular.

Before he'd even begun to punch in a number, both front doors of the other car opened and two men climbed out.

They sauntered over to the Mustang, and one of them tapped on Beth's window.

Her hand shaking, she rolled it down.

"Ms. Beth Gregory?" he asked.

She nodded.

"I'm police detective Rodger Ronalds. I'd like to go inside with you and ask you a few questions."

COLE COULD TELL that Rodger Ronalds and his partner weren't pleased when Beth said she wanted a lawyer present. But once he suggested heading to the nearest deli and picking up some lunch for them all, they began looking happier. And it wasn't long after they'd finished eating that Max Linsalle arrived.

The lawyer spent a few minutes talking privately

with Beth, then the two of them joined the police detectives in her office.

As soon as he was alone, Cole dug out Abbot's list of people the police had questioned after Larisa's murder. He didn't want to waste any time, because unless Glen Gregory was guilty, whoever had been trying to kill Beth was still walking around free.

Finding the name he wanted, he checked for it in the telephone directory. It wasn't there, so he plugged his laptop's modem into the phone jack and began accessing databases.

When he finally got some current data on the woman, he plugged the base of the cordless back in and punched in her office number.

"Dr. Rothstein's office," someone answered.

"Claire Delaney?" he said.

"Yes?"

"Ms. Delaney, my name is Cole Radford and I'm a private investigator."

"Yes?" she said again—suspiciously, this time.

"Ms. Delaney, I'd like to come and talk to you once you get home from work. It's extremely important."

"Oh, I'm sorry, but I'm busy tonight and—"

"It's extremely important to *you*," he interrupted, "that you talk to me before the police contact you."

"The police?" she said so quietly he knew she wasn't alone. "What's this about?"

"It's not something I can discuss over the phone. But I promise, you'll be very glad you talked to me first."

"I...well...all right. Do you know where I live?"

"The address I have is on Christie."

"Yes...well, I'll be there by five-thirty."

"Great. I'll see you then." Cole had barely put down the phone before he heard the door into the hallway open and close. A minute later, Beth and Max Linsalle appeared from her office.

"How did it go?" he asked them.

Beth's face was pale and she was clearly upset, but Max said, "Fine. Especially considering I had almost no time to prepare her."

"I told them I was certain my memory was wrong," she said. "But they took that with a grain of salt."

"Don't worry," Max told her. "When this comes to trial, your father's lawyer will call experts on recovered memories. And their job will be convincing the jury there's not a chance your memory's right."

"Trial." Beth slowly shook her head, as if she hadn't entirely come to terms with the fact her father had been charged.

"Well," Max said. "If you need me again, you know where to find me."

"Thanks," Cole said. "And thanks for getting here so quickly."

Once they showed Max out, Beth turned to Cole. She looked completely drained, and when he wrapped his arms around her she wordlessly rested her head against his shoulder.

He smoothed his hands down her back, the soft warmth of her body making him wish they could stay right here in her apartment. Telling himself they wouldn't be gone too long, he said, "We've got an appointment to get to."

"Oh?" She eased back a little and looked at him.

He smiled. "I wasn't just sitting around, you know. While you were playing twenty questions, I tracked down Claire Watkins, who's now Claire Delaney.''

Beth returned his smile with a wan one of her own. "And I'm supposed to ask who Claire Watkins Delaney is, right?"

"Right. You know, you're really catching on to this detective stuff."

"Very funny. So who is she?"

"She's your uncle's alibi. And we're going to go have a talk with her."

Chapter Fifteen

When they turned onto Claire Delaney's street, Beth's heart was in her throat.

"Are you sure we can't get thrown in jail for this?" she asked Cole. "Isn't it called entrapment or something?"

"Only when the police do it. When we do it, it's called bluffing."

"But I'm no good at bluffing."

"You don't have to be. I told you, all you have to do is follow my lead."

"I...Cole, maybe I should wait in the car and let you talk to her on your own."

"No, I need you. You're going to be what convinces her we're *not* bluffing."

"But what if I blow it?"

"You won't."

But what if she did?

Firmly, she told herself that she simply couldn't. If her uncle was guilty, his ex-secretary was probably the only person—aside from Mark himself—who knew he hadn't been in his office the entire morning Larisa was murdered.

But if she'd lied about it to the police back then,

how could Cole be so sure she'd tell *them* the truth now?

"This is it," he said, pulling up to the curb. "Ready?"

Beth nodded, even though she was anything but, and they climbed out of the car.

Claire Delaney opened the door almost before Cole knocked. An attractive, dark-haired woman in her late forties, she looked as anxious as Beth felt.

"Ms. Delaney?" Cole said, producing his investigator's license. "Cole Radford."

Claire eyed the ID closely, then looked at Beth. "And you're…?"

"She's the reason I have to talk to you," Cole said. "May we come in?"

With obvious reluctance, Claire led the way to her living room.

Once they were sitting down, Cole gestured toward Beth and said, "This is Beth Gregory."

The name didn't seem to mean anything until he added, "Dr. Mark Niebuhr's niece."

Claire sat up straighter in her chair. "You were the little girl who was in the house?"

Beth nodded, telling herself so far so good. But they hadn't reached the hard part yet.

"That…was a long time ago," Claire said. "It's been almost twenty years since I worked for Mark."

"And twenty-two since the murder," Cole said. "But why don't I cut straight to the chase? Can I assume you know something about the subject of recovered memories?"

Her gaze flickered to Beth, then back to Cole. "Yes, I've always worked for psychiatrists."

"Good, then I don't have to waste time explaining

the hows and whys. The bottom line is that Beth has remembered witnessing the murder.''

Claire's face paled. Then the corners of her mouth quirked, as if she thought he might be joking.

When neither Beth nor Cole said anything more, Claire finally looked at Beth. ''Remembering must have been…very traumatic.''

''It was.'' She took a deep breath and prayed she'd sound sincere. ''To suddenly remember seeing…to suddenly know that my uncle is a murderer… 'Very traumatic' doesn't begin to describe it.''

There was a deathly silence in the room. Beth had to fight the urge to babble on and fill it, but Cole had told her to say her lines and nothing more.

Claire slowly licked her lips. ''Your uncle?'' she said at last. ''You mean Larisa was murdered by a relative?''

''Ms. Delaney,'' Cole said, ''all three of us know which uncle Beth is referring to.''

''Excuse me? Don't try to tell me what I know, okay? I don't have a clue what you're talking about. The only one of her uncles I ever knew was Mark. And he certainly didn't do it. He was in his office, with me, when Larisa was murdered.''

''We know that's what you told the police. But let me fill you in on what's been happening recently.

''When Beth's memory surfaced, she didn't want to accuse her uncle on the basis of that alone. She realized she might be a victim of false memory syndrome. So I was hired to investigate the case—which is how I know what you told the police.

''And, as you're aware, after you gave Dr. Niebuhr an alibi, they didn't consider him a suspect. But because of Beth's recovered memory, I certainly did.

So I dug around in places that they never had. And I turned up proof the he *wasn't* in his office all morning.''

''What sort of *proof?*'' Claire demanded.

''Someone saw him in the middle of the morning. On Avenue Road, about halfway between his house and his office.''

''They must have been mistaken.''

Cole shook his head. ''It was actually two people. They were together when they saw him, and both of them knew him well. They wouldn't have mistaken anyone else for him.''

''You know how Mark had always been…so distinctive looking,'' Beth contributed. ''With his lion's mane of hair and all.'' That was her final line. The rest was up to Cole.

''Why didn't these people tell the police they'd seen him?'' Claire asked.

Beth tensed. There weren't any people, of course, which made this the weak link in their bluff. And if Cole's explanation didn't sound believable enough…

''Because the police didn't ask them,'' he said, his casual shrug implying the answer should have been obvious.

''As I said, once you gave Dr. Niebuhr his alibi, he wasn't a suspect. So they weren't looking for evidence that would implicate him. And when the newspapers requested help from the public, they asked anyone who'd seen a *stranger* in the vicinity of the murder to contact the police.''

Claire stared at Cole as if she wasn't sure whether he was being straight with her or not.

''Look,'' he said. ''I'm about to hand over the information I've gathered to the cops. If you tell me the truth about that morning, and I include it in my report, it'll be obvious that you've chosen to cooperate.

"I'm not trying to say that's as good as if you'd been honest way back then. But if you tell me the real story right now, it'll look better for you than if you were still sticking to your lie when I talked with you."

"And why should you care whether it looks better for me?"

Cole gave her another shrug. "Frankly, I don't. But we'll both benefit if you come clean now. I'm going to be dropping a virtually solved murder case in their laps. And every thread I've tied up for them, everything I've done that saves them effort, is going to earn me more brownie points. And in my line of work, I often need favors from the cops."

Beth held her breath while Claire eyed Cole and he eyed her back.

"You *don't* have a virtually solved murder case," she finally said. "Just because I gave Mark an alibi doesn't mean he killed his wife. And the fact those people saw him that morning doesn't, either."

Beth exhaled slowly. They still didn't have *proof* that Mark had murdered Larisa, but now they had both motive and opportunity. And between the journal, Cole's theory about how Mark had been the one to hide the murder weapon, and Claire's admission that she'd lied, surely the police would see that they'd arrested the wrong man.

But then they'd be arresting her uncle. A man she'd loved and trusted all her life. She blinked back tears as Claire finally broke the silence.

"Mark had a nine o'clock patient that morning,"

she said. "But then he was free until the afternoon. We'd blocked out the time for him to work on a paper he'd been invited to present at a conference.

"He had some research to do for it, though, so he couldn't work on it in his office. He had to go to the library. That's where he really was when Larisa was killed. But when the police came to the office in the afternoon, and told him Larisa was dead..."

"Yes?" Cole said.

"Well, before he left with them, he talked to me— asked me to swear that he'd been in the office all morning, working on the paper."

"Why?"

"He said he knew that in a murder case, the husband is always the primary suspect. And that he hadn't seen anyone he knew at the library, and he doubted anyone there would have noticed him. He said he'd just slipped into the stacks and worked on his own in one of the carrels."

"He said no one would have noticed him? But he's the type of man that people always notice."

"Well...yes."

"Then why did you lie? Why didn't you point out that *someone* would remember seeing him there? And tell him that you weren't going to cover for him?"

Claire shrugged.

"You must have had a reason," Cole pressed. "People don't perjure themselves for the fun of it."

She hesitated, then said, "All right, I had a reason. I was in love with him. We'd been involved for about a year, and when he asked me to make things easier for him..."

Beth bit her lip as an image of Larisa appeared in

her mind's eye. Mark had killed her because she'd been having an affair, when at the very same time he'd been having one of his own. There was just so much in the world that wasn't right.

"Look, I know how horrible this is going to sound," Claire continued, "but when I heard Larisa was dead, the first thing I thought was that now Mark and I could get married.

"We didn't, of course. He…we broke things off a couple of years later—which was when I went looking for a new job. But, at the time, when he asked me to tell a little white lie, I didn't see how it could hurt. Not when I knew he hadn't killed her.

"You were right to realize you could be a victim of false memory syndrome," she added to Beth. "Because if you remember Mark as the killer, your memory *is* wrong. I could never have been in love with a man who was capable of murder."

"HE *WAS* CAPABLE OF MURDER," Beth murmured as they headed back to Cole's car. After being close to Mark for so many years, she was having a lot of trouble coming to terms with that. But she simply knew, deep down, that he had been the one. And saying the words out loud made it a little more real.

"You're remembering the true killer's face now? And it was Mark?"

"No. Not exactly. But you know how I've been insisting, all along, that the image of my father couldn't be right?"

"Uh-huh."

"Well, my memory still isn't picturing Mark as the killer. But when I imagine him standing there with the knife… That image seems right. I mean, as much as I hate that it does, it's a fact. So doesn't that have to mean he did it?''

Cole reached for her hand. ''I doubt the police would buy it as proof positive. But Mark said your memory would probably grow more detailed over time. So if that happens... Or maybe you should talk to somebody. Another psychiatrist—one who's worked with other people who've recovered memories. One who could help you sort things out.''

''I think you're right. But in the meantime,'' she added as they got into the car, ''do we have enough that they'll release my father?''

''I hope so.'' Cole started the engine and pulled away from the curb.

''You mean you don't think so?'' she pressed when he offered nothing more.

''I just don't know, but you shouldn't count on it.''

She tried to fight off her disappointment. She'd pretty well convinced herself that she *could* count on it.

''Remember when you and Mark first came to see me?'' Cole continued. ''How you were talking about the police having tunnel vision?''

''Uh-huh.''

''Well, you were right. Sometimes they do. And at the moment, they're sitting with a pretty solid circumstantial case against your father.

''Your mother had a key to the Niebuhrs', which she couldn't account for at the time of the murder. Obviously, he could have taken it. And the murder weapon was hidden in the wall of his house. Plus, there's Mark's suggesting that your father and Larisa might have restarted their affair, which might have led to a crime of passion.''

Beth shook her head. Her father having an affair with Larisa was something else she was having trouble coming to terms with.

Telling herself not to think about that for the moment, she said, ''But you're sounding as if the police might not believe it was Mark. How couldn't they when we've got the journal now? And when Claire's admitted she lied? Doesn't that change the picture entirely?''

''It depends on how they view things. On whether they figure Mark actually read the journal and knew Larisa was planning to leave him. And whether they think there's a good chance he really was at the library. At any rate, as far as your father's concerned, they might keep him in custody at least until they get the DNA test results on the knife.''

''How long will that be?''

''Oh, probably five or six weeks.''

Beth closed her eyes, trying not to think about her father being in jail for another five or six weeks. Or, worse yet, Cole had said ''at least.'' And if the police had a serious case of tunnel vision...

''You know,'' he continued, ''I think I've finally figured out why your uncle seems so obsessed with Larisa's memory.''

''Oh?''

He nodded. ''Guilt. He's never really come to terms with the fact that he murdered her, and he's trying to make atonement.''

She forced a smile. ''Maybe *you* should have been a psychiatrist.''

They didn't talk much the rest of the way home,

but after he'd parked outside her apartment, Cole said, "As soon as we go in, I'll write up everything for the police. But once we give them my report and the journal, it's up to them how they proceed. And how quickly.

"I...dammit, Beth, I guess here I go scaring you again, but even if your uncle *is* guilty, there's no saying how long he'll still be walking around free. And if they decide our evidence isn't enough to prosecute on and they can't turn up anything more, they won't even charge him."

Her throat was suddenly tight. "You *are* scaring me again. What if that happens? Would they keep on trying to railroad my father? And if Mark was free, I'd be left worrying forever, wouldn't I?"

Cole rested his fingers against her cheek. "I've been thinking about that. And it seems to me that your having a long-term bodyguard would be a good idea."

She gazed at him, trying to determine exactly what he was saying, afraid she was reading too much into his words. "I couldn't afford one for *very* long term," she said at last.

"Well, I was thinking more along the lines of a volunteer." He gave her a to-die-for smile that sent even the worst of her worries scurrying into the darkest recesses of her mind.

"Were you thinking about any particular volunteer?" she murmured.

"What do you think?" he said, leaning closer to kiss her.

It was such a hot, hard, possessing kiss that she could feel every bone in her body melting.

"Why don't we move this inside," he finally

whispered. "And I'll leave writing things up until later."

He took his gun out of the glove compartment and tucked it against the small of his back, slinging his suit jacket over his shoulder to conceal it when they got out of the car.

Once they'd headed into her building and the elevator door closed behind them, he began kissing her again. By the time they reached her apartment, all she could think about was making love.

They raced through her office, then she stopped in her tracks. Her mother was sitting in the living room, looking decidedly glassy-eyed, as if she'd taken more of her anxiety pills than was safe.

Cole froze beside Beth, gut instinct telling him there was a whole lot wrong with this picture—in addition to Angela's looking spaced out. And he knew his instinct was right when Beth said, "Mom? How did you get in? You don't have a key."

He nonchalantly tossed his jacket over a dining room chair, trying to look as if he didn't think anything was wrong. But what the hell was the deal? Had his off-the-wall suspicions been right, after all? Had *Angela* killed Larisa?

He began praying that wasn't it, because he didn't know how Beth could handle it.

"I came to get Larisa's journal. I—"

"Mom? How did you know I had it?"

Cole could feel his gun pressed against his back, and he couldn't help thinking that Angela might have a weapon.

"Mark told me."

"But how did *he* know?"

"That old neighbor." Angela vaguely waved her

hand. "Miss Boise or something. No, that's not right. I'll—"

"Angela?" Cole said quietly. "Her name's not important. But tell us why you came for the journal."

"Why…because Mark said Beth wanted him to pick it up. But she forgot to tell him exactly where it was. So he thought it would be better if I came and found it, because she might not want him rummaging through her apartment."

"But how did you get a key?" Beth asked.

When Angela merely gazed at her blankly, she said, "Mom, I want you to go and lie down in the bedroom, okay?"

"No, I have to—"

"You don't have to do anything. I think you took too many of your pills, and the best thing you can do is sleep for a while."

"You're sure that's the best thing?" Cole said.

Beth nodded. "The first time we went through this, I called her doctor for advice. Come on," she added, turning back to her mother.

"But I—"

"Come on." She helped Angela up off the couch and led her into the bedroom.

A minute later, she came back out and closed the door. "I'm going to call her doctor again, the first chance I get. She shouldn't have enough of those damn pills around to make her that woozy. She fell asleep the second her head hit the pillow."

"Don't blame her doctor," Mark said from behind them. "And I've got a gun, so don't either of you move," he snapped as Cole started to turn.

A second later, he felt Mark taking his gun from his waistband.

"I gave her the pills," Mark explained. "She showed up at my office, all upset, and I had to calm her down. Now, you two go sit on the couch."

Once they had, Beth said, "Mark?"

She sounded scared to death.

"It was you who had a key to my apartment, wasn't it?" she said. "How did you get it?"

"You have to ask? You, who has to carry spare keys because you're always misplacing them? You left them at my apartment a while back, and I had them copied—just in case."

"Just in case you wanted to come here and kill me?" she whispered. "Have you always intended to kill me if I started to remember? Ever since I was a child? Is that why you stayed close to Mom and me all these years?"

"Beth, I never *wanted* to kill you."

Cole resisted asking why, if that was true, he'd hired those shooters.

"I just brought your mother up here to find the journal," Mark continued. "While I waited in the car and kept an eye out for you. And if she'd only been in here a few minutes, instead of half an hour..."

As Mark's words trailed off, Cole eyed the good doctor, wondering if Beth was seeing what he was— not a loving uncle but a man with such a cold, deadly look in his eyes that getting out of this alive might be an impossibility.

But it couldn't be. He couldn't lose Beth when he'd barely found her.

"Let's go back to the point here," Mark said. "Where's the journal?"

"We don't have the damn journal," Cole said before Beth could reply.

"Don't play games! Esther Voise told me the whole story. I was curious about what she'd said to you the other day, so I dropped by her house. I figured I'd tell her that you'd mentioned seeing her, and it had made me think about paying her a visit for old times' sake.

"But it turned out I didn't have to give her any explanation. She assumed I was there to thank her for helping you two get the journal for me. Now, where is it?"

"We've already given it to the police," Cole said.

"Oh? Then I guess there's no reason not to kill you both. Right now."

"You'd never get away with it."

"No? Given the shape Angela's in, I think I will. I can make it look as if *she* killed you—then set fire to the place."

Cole exhaled slowly, aware that just might work. Then, telling himself there was nothing to do but stall for time and pray for a miracle, he said, "If you're going to kill us, why would we give you the journal? Even if we still had it?"

"All right…I guess there are a few ways we can play this. For starters, I could put a couple of bullets in Beth, and see if you're *still* telling me the police already have it."

Beth glanced at Cole, the taste of terror bitter in her mouth.

He muttered something under his breath, then said, "It's in her office."

"That's better. Let's go and get it."

"Can I ask you one question first?"

Mark hesitated, then said, "One."

"Was it really worth murdering Larisa to keep her from leaving you?"

He slowly shook his head. "She wasn't planning to just leave me. I had a lot of assets in her name— for tax purposes. And after I read the journal, I checked on them.

"She'd been liquidating them. She wasn't planning on running off with Roth poor. She was going to do it with my money."

"But—"

"That was your one question, so let's go."

Single file, they headed into the office, Beth's heart pounding.

"We stashed it behind the bookcase," Cole said.

"Not very original."

"Yeah, well, I wasn't in a very original frame of mind. But it took two of us to move the thing, so I'm going to need some help."

Beth stood looking everywhere but at Mark, afraid that if he caught her gaze he'd realize something was up. Cole knew as well as she did that the journal was locked in her desk, which had to mean he had a plan. She just hoped with all her heart it was a good one.

He walked over to the bookcase, pulled an armload of books off a shelf and piled them on her desk.

"This would go faster if you gave me a hand," he told Mark.

"Sure. And you'd probably like it if I asked Beth to hold the gun, too. Help him," he added, to her.

She began moving books, desperately wishing she knew what Cole had in mind.

"We'd better get the paperweights down before

we fill up the desk,'' he said, shooting her a quick glance.

Her pulse began doing triple time. Whatever he was going to try, he was going to do it now.

''Shove some of those books closer to the edge,'' he told her, nodding toward the desk. ''Make room for these,'' he added, reaching for a couple of the largest paperweights.

She turned toward the desk, her mind racing. What could she do to help?

Shove some of those books closer to the edge.

Oh, Lord, she'd almost missed what he'd been trying to tell her. Zeroing in on one of the highest stacks, she gave it a push that sent it tumbling toward the floor.

After that, everything happened so fast there was barely time for her brain to register it.

Mark glanced toward the falling books. Something flew across the room. It struck the side of his head, he staggered off balance, and her office exploded with a deafening sound. Then Cole tackled Mark and they both went down.

Seconds later, Cole had his knee in the small of Mark's back, had Mark's hands pinned to the floor above his head, and was telling her to get the gun.

Looking quickly around, she spotted it under the desk. She scooped it up and wheeled back toward the men, relief flooding her when she saw that Mark wasn't even trying to struggle.

Then she realized he was barely conscious. And that there was an angry-looking lump forming on the side of his head—that what had flown across the room and hit him was one of her paperweights.

For another few moments, she simply stood gazing

down at the two of them, not sure if she felt more like laughing or crying. Mark, whom she'd trusted from childhood, had wanted to kill her. Cole, whom she'd known for barely any time at all, had saved her life.

And now everything in her world would be getting back to normal. Which meant that laughing made a lot more sense than crying.

"Nice going." Cole nodded toward the books scattered on the floor.

She smiled, amazed at how easy it suddenly was.

THE FOLLOWING EVENING, once they'd finished celebrating Beth's father's release with champagne, he said, "I guess I can't thank you two any more than I already have. But if it hadn't been for you..."

Leaving it at that, he stood up. "I've got to head home and get some sleep. You'd never believe how noisy a jail is at night."

Beth and Cole walked him out through the office, then he reached for her and gave her a long, hard hug. "I'm sorry you had to learn about Larisa and me," he whispered. "I've never been able to forgive myself for being that weak. I just hope you'll be able to."

"I'm going to try," she whispered back.

"Good. Let's start working on putting the past behind us."

She nodded, but it would be a long time before they'd really be able to do that. They'd all have to testify at Mark's trial, and until that was over and done with...

"I'll call you soon," he said.

She gave him another hug, then he shook hands with Cole and was gone.

"You know, I could use one of those hugs," Cole told her.

Wrapping her arms around him, she held him tightly, feeling a little uncertain about where things were going from here.

Oh, she knew with all her heart what *she* wanted. She'd never fallen in love like this before—neither as quickly nor as deeply. But did Cole have the same, insane, "want to be with this person every second" feeling about her that she had about him?

"We haven't had much chance to talk in the last twenty-four hours," he said.

"I noticed," she murmured. They'd spent until late last night with Rodger Ronalds and his partner. And by the time the detectives left, she and Cole had been talked out. All they'd wanted to do was make love, then fall asleep in each other's arms. And today they'd spent the entire day at police headquarters.

"So, let's talk now." Taking her hand, Cole led her back into the living room.

She snuggled down beside him on the couch, telling herself not to be uneasy about what this talk might entail. But when he said, "I guess you don't need a live-in bodyguard anymore," her heart stood still.

His words meant that he'd be going back to his own apartment tonight. And if he was content to leave, he didn't have that same feeling she had.

Tears filling her eyes, she gathered up every ounce of her self-control. "No, I guess, from now on, I'll be safe without a bodyguard."

"Then...well, hell, Beth, if I can't use that as an

excuse to stay here permanently, I was thinking that maybe we should get married.''

For half a second, she was sure she'd misheard him. Then the happiness bubbling up inside her put the champagne bubbles to shame.

''I mean, I realize this has been awfully fast,'' he continued. ''But I couldn't love you any more if we'd known each other for a hundred years. So...what do you say?''

''I say yes,'' she whispered.

She'd have said more if he hadn't started kissing her.

But that was all right. Sometimes, there were better ways to say things than with words.

'HAVE I DONE something wrong?' Angie persisted, wishing Taylor would emit a sense of camaraderie instead of holding an impenetrable reserve.

'Not at all,' he assured her. 'I would say a lot of things right. You seem to be fitting into our little Outback community very well. I've heard only good things about you.'

'They're nice people,' she said sincerely. Only the Maguire family kept her shut out of their hearts.

'Yes,' he agreed. 'Though I appreciate it's taken considerable effort from you. It is a world away from what you're used to.'

The control Angie had been exerting over her feelings snapped. He wasn't as blatant as his aunt in his prejudice against her but she'd felt it coming through every word he'd spoken and she didn't deserve any of it.

'Don't judge me by your wife!'

His jaw jerked. A flicker of some dark emotion destroyed the steady power of his probing gaze.

'No two people are the same. If you don't know that, you're a man of very limited vision. So I come from the city as your wife did! That doesn't stop me from being an individual in my own right.'

She straightened up, proudly defiant, furiously angry with the situation. 'I'm *me*. Angie Cordell. And it's time you took the blinkers off your eyes, Taylor Maguire.'

Then she whirled away from him, too agitated by the explosive expulsion of her emotion to keep facing him.

The storm outside hadn't yet eased. There was nowhere to go. She stopped at the window, staring blindly at the torrential rain. The thundering on the roof was almost deafening but it wasn't as loud as the silence behind her.

'You want me to go, don't you? You've given me a month's respite and now you want me to leave and channel my energies somewhere else.'

'I didn't say that, Angie.'

'You were working your way around it.' Bitterness at his tactics spewed the suspicion. 'Do you have your first choice of governess waiting in the wings?'

'No. I said I'd give you a chance.'

'Have you?' She swung around to face him. 'Have you really, Taylor?'

He hadn't moved. He didn't move now except to make a gesture of appeasement. 'Angie, I was merely trying to ascertain how you felt.'

'Then let me tell you your cynicism was shining through every word.'

He frowned, shook his head. 'I didn't mean to hurt you.' The blue eyes fastened on hers with devastating sincerity. 'I truly did not come in here to take you down or suggest you leave.'

Her heart jiggled painfully. He might be speaking the truth but the judgements were still there, the judgements that ruled his attitude towards her, that kept her shut out of his life, denied any real sharing with him, denied his confidence and trust. She didn't know why it meant so much to her but it did. It did. And the need to fight for justice from him was as much a raging torrent inside her as the rain outside.

DEBBIE MACOMBER

invites you to the

★ ★ ★ HEART OF TEXAS ★ ★ ★

Join Debbie Macomber as she brings you the lives
and loves of the folks in the ranching community
of Promise, Texas.

If you loved Midnight Sons—don't miss
Heart of Texas! A brand-new six-book series
from Debbie Macomber.

Available in February 1998
at your favorite retail store.

Heart of Texas by Debbie Macomber

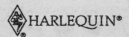

HARLEQUIN®

MEN at WORK
All work and no play? Not these men!

April 1998
KNIGHT SPARKS by Mary Lynn Baxter
Sexy lawman Rance Knight made a career of arresting the bad guys. Somehow, though, he thought policewoman Carly Mitchum was framed. Once they'd uncovered the truth, could Rance let Carly go...or would he make a citizen's arrest?

May 1998
HOODWINKED by Diana Palmer
CEO Jake Edwards donned coveralls and went undercover as a mechanic to find the saboteur in his company. Nothing—or no one—would distract him, not even beautiful secretary Maureen Harris. Jake had to catch the thief—*and* the woman who'd stolen his heart!

June 1998
DEFYING GRAVITY by Rachel Lee
Tim O'Shaughnessy and his business partner, Liz Pennington, had always been close—but never *this* close. As the danger of their assignment escalated, so did their passion. When the job was over, could they ever go back to business as usual?

MEN AT WORK™

Available at your favorite retail outlet!

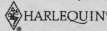 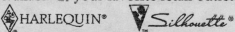

Look us up on-line at: http://www.romance.net   PMAW1

HARLEQUIN ULTIMATE GUIDES™

A series of how-to books for today's woman.

Act now to order some of these extremely
helpful guides just for you!

*Whatever the situation, Harlequin Ultimate Guides™
has all the answers!*

#80507	HOW TO TALK TO A	$4.99 U.S. ☐	
	NAKED MAN	$5.50 CAN.☐	
#80508	I CAN FIX THAT	$5.99 U.S. ☐	
		$6.99 CAN.☐	
#80510	WHAT YOUR TRAVEL AGENT	$5.99 U.S. ☐	
	KNOWS THAT YOU DON'T	$6.99 CAN.☐	
#80511	RISING TO THE OCCASION		
	More Than Manners: Real Life	$5.99 U.S. ☐	
	Etiquette for Today's Woman	$6.99 CAN.☐	
#80513	WHAT GREAT CHEFS	$5.99 U.S. ☐	
	KNOW THAT YOU DON'T	$6.99 CAN.☐	
#80514	WHAT SAVVY INVESTORS	$5.99 U.S. ☐	
	KNOW THAT YOU DON'T	$6.99 CAN.☐	
#80509	GET WHAT YOU WANT OUT OF	$5.99 U.S. ☐	
	LIFE—AND KEEP IT!	$6.99 CAN.☐	

(quantities may be limited on some titles)

TOTAL AMOUNT	$
POSTAGE & HANDLING	$

($1.00 for one book, 50¢ for each additional)

APPLICABLE TAXES*	$ _____
TOTAL PAYABLE	$ _____

(check or money order—please do not send cash)

To order, complete this form and send it, along with a check or money
order for the total above, payable to Harlequin Ultimate Guides, to:
In the U.S.: 3010 Walden Avenue, P.O. Box 9047, Buffalo, NY
14269-9047; **In Canada:** P.O. Box 613, Fort Erie, Ontario, L2A 5X3.

Name: _____

Address: _____ City: _____

State/Prov.: _____ Zip/Postal Code: _____

*New York residents remit applicable sales taxes.
Canadian residents remit applicable GST and provincial taxes.

HARLEQUIN®

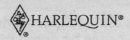 HARLEQUIN®

Not The Same Old Story!

 HARLEQUIN PRESENTS®
Exciting, glamorous romance stories that take readers around the world.

 Harlequin Romance®
Sparkling, fresh and tender love stories that bring you pure romance.

 HARLEQUIN® Temptation
Bold and adventurous—Temptation is strong women, bad boys, great sex!

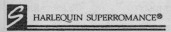 HARLEQUIN SUPERROMANCE®
Provocative and realistic stories that celebrate life and love.

 HARLEQUIN® AMERICAN ROMANCE®
Contemporary fairy tales—where anything is possible and where dreams come true.

 HARLEQUIN® INTRIGUE®
Heart-stopping, suspenseful adventures that combine the best of romance and mystery.

 LOVE & LAUGHTER™
Humorous and romantic stories that capture the lighter side of love.

Heat up your summer this July with

Summer Lovers

This July, bestselling authors Barbara Delinsky, Elizabeth Lowell and Anne Stuart present three couples with pasts that threaten their future happiness. Can they play with fire without being burned?

FIRST, BEST AND ONLY
by Barbara Delinsky

GRANITE MAN
by Elizabeth Lowell

CHAIN OF LOVE
by Anne Stuart

Available wherever Harlequin and Silhouette books are sold.

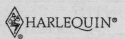HARLEQUIN®

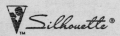Silhouette®

HREQ798

COMING NEXT MONTH

#473 NOWHERE MAN by Rebecca York
43 Light St.
Kathryn Kelley escaped a stalker only to find herself in more trouble
when she agreed to help a dangerous volunteer for a secret mission.
A striking physical specimen, Hunter was dangerous, all right...to
her heart.

#474 TRUE HEARTS by Maggie Ferguson
When her parents died suddenly, Hailey Monroe learned she was
adopted. But when security consultant Sean Cassadine sweeps into
her life, insisting she needs his protection, he tells a more surprising
tale—her real name is Susan Palmer, and as a baby, she was kid-
napped....

#475 FUGITIVE FATHER by Jean Barrett
Noah Rhyder lost his freedom and custody of his son to an unjust
murder conviction. Now on the run, he'll do anything to get his
son back, including kidnap Joel's foster mother. But when
Ellie Mathieson tells him Joel has been sent away, Noah needs her
help more than ever—for his son could be with the real murderer....

#476 THE ONLY MAN TO TRUST by Grace Green
Her Protector
Blair Enderby never dreamed she'd be summoned to Matt Straith's
estate or that he was still in love with her...or that someone wanted
to frame Matt and steal his millions. Everyone at the estate had motive,
and Matt vowed to keep Blair from harm. He'd lost her once and no
madman would destroy their future now....

AVAILABLE THIS MONTH:

#469 REMEMBER MY TOUCH
Gayle Wilson

#470 THE MISSING HOUR
Dawn Stewardson

**#471 JODIE'S LITTLE
SECRETS**
Joanna Wayne

#472 RUNAWAY HEART
Saranne Dawson

Look us up on-line at: http://www.romance.net